DANGER
TO OTHERS

Martha Crites

NORTH WEST CORNER BOOKS

Kenmore, WA

Northwest Corner Books published by Epicenter Press

Epicenter Press
6524 NE 181st St. Suite 2
Kenmore, WA 98028.
www.Epicenterpress.com
www.Coffeetownpress.com
www.Camelpress.com

For more information go to: www.Epicenterpress.com
Author Website: https://marthacrites.com/

Danger To Others
Copyright © 2022 by Martha Crites

ISBN: 9781942078777 (trade paper)
ISBN: 9781945078784 (ebook)

Printed in the United States of America

Dedication

In honor of my grandmother, Helen Baxter Crites

Acknowledgments

I owe thanks to so many people for their help in the writing of this book. First, and most tolerant, is my husband, Jim Limardi, reader extraordinaire.

Thanks also to my writing group: Linda Anderson, Rachel Bukey, Curt Colbert, and Janis Wildy for many years of listening over quiche and later, over Zoom. I am indebted to Roger Midget and Flip O'Reilly for their information about Crisis and Commitment Services; Leisa Wright, psychiatric nurse, for her stories about testifying in court cases. All mistakes are mine. Rachel, Roger and Janice also contributed close reading and insight into story structure. Catherine Smith added her careful editing. Thanks to Carol Miller who transcribed and shared my aunt's diaries with me. They shed a little light on the death of my grandmother, Helen.

I started writing *Danger to Others* for Waverly Fitzgerald who had enough faith in me to publish my first novel. Waverly died before I finished this book, but I will always be grateful for her support. My thanks now go to Phil Garrett of Epicenter Press/ Northwest Corner Books for taking a chance on me.

Finally, I am always indebted to the staff and patients of Harborview Medical Center. They have enriched my life.

February 2

My work partner, Annie Bartoz, and I leave the white county-owned Ford sedan down the block. We are here to evaluate Calvin Cole, a suicidal, 43-year-old who lives with his parents. Our paperwork reports his recent visit to a hospital emergency room, citing as issues depression and paranoia. No legal history, no known weapons. This is what I remember: Late afternoon. Light slants from broken clouds in the west and two crows cawing from an electrical wire in front of a small wooden bungalow in Seattle's Ballard neighborhood.

Inside, Cole's parents stand to greet us, their matching brown recliners still rocking after they are up. The cramped living room has a beige carpet, flattened, and stained from heavy use. A narrow hallway leads to bedrooms on one side and the bathroom at the far end.

I tell them, "My name is Grace Vaccaro. My partner, Annie Bartoz, and I work for King County." I explain our roles as mental health evaluators, telling them we'll offer voluntary treatment first.

"He moved back home when he lost his job," his mother says. "He was depressed, so he stayed in his room and drank."

She hadn't said this in the phone intake interview. Alcohol could make him impulsive. Now she tells us he's threatened her. I ask where Calvin is. In the bathroom, she tells us, and he won't come out. Annie and I make eye contact. We've gotten each other out of some tight spots, and sometimes we don't have to put our thoughts into words. We know this evaluation is going downhill fast.

We step outside and decide to get police backup to be safe. Half an hour later, we're back with the officers. We've worked with Nate Fischer once before. He's well over six feet tall and seems just as wide. The other officer is new to us, a young man with eyebrows that go up and down when he talks.

Annie and I guide the parents outside. Before we're out the door, I see the officers approach the bathroom, talking calmly, but their hands are near their guns. Nate takes up all the space.

"Let me talk to him." The mother screams and runs inside.

That's when all hell breaks loose. Annie and I move to divert her. The bathroom door flies open. The tiny house explodes with gunfire. I see it in slow motion. Calvin Cole, balding and unshaven in a gray t-shirt and jeans a size too big from weight loss, flies forward, a gun flashing. Nate is propelled back. Before he's down the other officer fires and Cole drops. I run and rip off my jacket to apply pressure where Nate's shoulder blooms red. The mother climbs over us both to reach her son, also down. Her Nikes strike my face and Nate's chest.

The other officer radios for help.

This is not our usual day. This is not the story I wanted to tell.

Chapter 1

Snowberry bushes, studded with the white fruits Native People called corpse berries, had filled in an abandoned path. I pushed through to the creek and found a clearing by a cedar snag. We'd left the broken tree to shelter wildlife. Black-hooded juncos fluttered in the underbrush. I remembered when my mother used to bring me here to play. By the time we got to the creek's edge, the box of Mom's ashes felt heavier than they really were. I reached in and took a handful, but when I released it, the chill morning wind changed and blew ash into my face. I wiped my stinging eyes, turned for better aim and let go another handful. Mom had died in February, after a few short weeks of illness—pneumonia, followed by a heart attack. Years of smoking caught up with her in her seventies. It was just a week after the evaluation that ended in a shooting. We'd had a memorial with family and friends, but her ashes had lingered on a shelf in the living room until now, late October.

My daughter Nell brightened the woods in her puffy chartreuse coat, no funeral colors for her. The wind blew strands of dark hair across her face. She pulled it into a ponytail and spread the next handful of ash into the creek.

"Grandma Rose will get to travel," she said. Nell was the one who had pushed me to scatter the ashes. She graduated from college a year ago and had moved back home to save for a big adventure. Now she was about to leave for 3 months in Europe. She was afraid the box would collect more dust by the time she got home. I couldn't put this off any longer, so we'd chosen today, Mom's birthday.

"Rose wasn't much for traveling," Frank said and pushed up the sleeves of his jacket taking the next turn, "but the creek won't take her far."

I tapped out the final remains and held my hands in the biting creek water until they felt numb. All in silence. I'd come today without a ceremony. I was saying good-bye in the worst possible way and didn't know why. But I did know. Stoicism was how I operated. I set my reactions aside, no matter what happened.

Frank and Nell rinsed their hands too, then went ahead to our house through the fern-lined woods. The duff of fallen leaves padded my footsteps and the overripe smell of autumn hung in the air. I walked more slowly past Nell's shingled cottage, separated from the main house by a Japanese garden. I paused at the fan-shaped leaves of two ginkgoes shimmering yellow against the blue autumn sky. They'd been planted to honor my grandparents' deaths. A pair of ravens rocked and croaked their throaty call from the cottage roof, reminding me of the crows outside the Cole house. It had been a rough nine months.

I let myself in the back door. Frank and I had moved to my grandparents' house when they died. The long commute from Duvall to Seattle was frustrating but living in the country always renewed me.

Inside the house, Caesar our husky, spun and bumped my legs, indignant that I'd been on a walk without him. Frank and Nell had already started cooking breakfast.

"Dad went into town for bacon before you even got up," Nell said. She cocked her hip while she stirred pancake batter in a sky-blue, enamel bowl we'd found at a yard sale. "I read that book on grief you left lying around. It said to do three things: have a ceremony, wash your hands, then eat. We already did the first two." Mustard-colored jeans hugged her hips, and a hand-knit sweater didn't reach her belt line. People said we looked alike, but at Nell's age, her dark eyes and hair had a glow. The word nubile came to mind. She hadn't been dating anyone lately—she didn't want ties right now.

I draped my arm around her shoulder. "It wasn't much of a ceremony. Thanks for taking over."

"We knew you'd be tired after working the night shift," Frank said and pulled an apron over his head. This morning, he wore a loose-fitting rayon shirt and his good pair of jeans. I was touched that he'd gotten dressed up to walk through the woods for our private ceremony.

With his tall and narrow build, clothes hung on him in a way I envied. Nell has inherited her father's build too. His salt and pepper hair had turned white at the temples, a nice contrast with his still tan face.

The kitchen took on the smoky scent of sizzling bacon. I set the table and cut a single late rose for a handblown vase. My phone buzzed in my pocket and the screen read *Annie*. I silenced it and set it on the table, vowing to call after breakfast.

When Frank, and Nell, and I sat down to eat, the stories came naturally.

"Nell, when you were about three, Rose was the only person who could get you to take a bath," Frank said before swallowing a big bite. "And the pancakes are delicious."

"Grandma Rose's favorite."

Nell was right about that, but I don't think I'd told her it was one of the first meals I'd learned to make as a girl when Mom—her Grandma Rose—was depressed and stopped cooking. My feelings about this ceremonial meal were mixed. I set that aside, though, in favor of other memories.

"The first time she met your dad," I said, "She said he was the man I was going to marry."

Frank laughed. "You were so oppositional, you said you'd be a spinster for life."

The house was warm, and we sat with our elbows on the dark oak table. Nell told about how my mom would bend over her sewing machine with a cigarette clamped between her lips while the ash grew long, but never fell on her work.

The phone buzzed again, and I said, "Later," as if Annie could hear me. The pancakes were dense and sweet in counterpoint to the crunch and salt of the bacon, so much better than the taste of my childhood attempts at cooking. I reached for a second serving and my phone pinged a single note. I wouldn't interrupt our meal to talk to anyone, but I peeked to read the text. It was Annie: *A woman you evaluated last night says she murdered her therapist.* I swallowed hard, then excused myself and called.

I knew who Annie meant right away—the only one with a therapist. "I don't believe Laurel killed anyone," Annie said, sounding troubled. Neither of us had fared well since the shooting. We often evaluated people who were a danger, but together, we used our skills to keep everyone safe. Nothing like the Cole shooting had happened in years, long before we'd joined the evaluation team.

Leaving the ritual breakfast for my mom seemed wrong, but Frank and Nell insisted, because as the person who assessed the young woman, I had begun to wonder if I'd missed something.

When I went to get ready, Nell was in the bathroom putting on a touch of makeup.

"Where are you off to?" I was rushing to brush my teeth, so we shared the sink.

"I'm meeting my supervisor. I'm excited about the trip, but I hate leaving my job. Wouldn't it be great if they'll let me come back to work afterwards?"

Nell already worked as a Spanish interpreter with a group of low-income clinics, a rare achievement for a young, nonnative speaker. But the older, Latino interpreters had taken her under their collective wing and encouraged her. Nell's trip to Europe would have two parts. First, she would visit Gwen, my best friend who had bought a house in the south of France and moved there to restore it. Then Nell would attend an advanced medical Spanish class in Salamanca, Spain. I wasn't thrilled about her leaving. I already missed having Gwen to talk and laugh with. I was afraid Nell might decide to settle abroad too. Her desire to come back to her job was good news indeed.

"Great," I responded, licking my finger, and wiping a stray speck of mascara from her cheek. "Who do you talk to?"

She pulled away at my touch—almost imperceptibly, then relaxed. The push and pull of Nell's moving into adulthood had lessened these days, but her move home to save for the trip sometimes brought it back. She was in a good mood though and swatted my hand away. "Grandma Rose never stopped doing the spit-wipe either. At least you don't have cigarette breath. I see the clinic supervisor, he's an administrator, not one of the regular staff."

"He's in on Saturdays?"

"Not usually, but I guess he is today." We finished our primping and grabbed our coats.

I hurried Nell out to the old Toyota truck she'd accepted from me as a hand-me-down and gave her a quick hug before she climbed in. She responded by holding on a long time.

"Good luck," I told her.

"Good luck with the woman you evaluated," she said, and I pushed the door closed after her. The hinge on the truck needed grease and groaned—metal on metal—when I pushed it shut. Then I climbed into the new Prius that assuaged my guilt about my long commute into the city.

I replayed the case on my way into the city to meet Annie. The drive would take an hour in light mid-day traffic. I'd made it a million times. So, I tried to remember everything I could as I sped over the bridge crossing the Snoqualmie River and into the trees lining Woodinville-Duvall Road. Laurel James was young and smart, the kind of person I hoped to see get better. The kind who could disappoint me. Had she killed her therapist? Now the things I'd seen as delusion took on a different light.

I'd had two referrals from Harborview's Psychiatric Emergency Services the night before. In the world of medical acronyms, it was shortened to the PES, and pronounced with a Z, like the Pez candy dispensers. After arriving, I waited outside the locked metal door for someone to buzz me in. A closed-circuit screen gave a view of a short hallway. Before the camera installation, patients occasionally fled by hovering unseen at the exit. On the screen, a row of doors lined the right side of the hall, a couple patients clustered at a tv on the left. Safe to enter when the lock buzzed for me to enter.

Walking to the office, I had glanced in an open door, guessing the young woman inside was someone I'd be seeing. She rocked back and forth on a gurney. The activity around her made me shake my head. Two doctors, probably still in residency, and a middle-aged woman with spiky platinum hair and a pressed chef's jacket crowded the narrow room. The young woman's voice rose over theirs, singing "a tisket, a tasket I really need a casket." People say all kinds of things in a psychiatric crisis. I didn't take it to mean that she had killed someone, and I always ask about homicidal ideation.

Shandra, a nurse I'd known for years, had met me in the hall. "Grace! I'm glad you're here," she whispered under her breath, even though no one was paying any attention to us. She walked me to the brightly lit office to brief me.

"Is that one of my evals?" I asked.

"Yes. They're driving me crazy." She put out her left hand, palm up and explained, "That woman is the mother, and she won't stop hovering." In an on-the-other-hand move, she turned up the right, "The girl sliced her arms, and the medicine docs won't examine her until Mom leaves. Mom won't leave. I was just about to get pushy. Now that you are here, maybe you could collect some family history." A few weeks ago, Shandra had cut off her dreadlocks and the effect made her look softer, but she wasn't the type to take any guff from family members or young doctors.

She swiped dramatically at her short gray afro.

"And get her out of your hair?" I said. "Sure. I may need her statement for the detention." I rolled my shoulders to unkink them, and ward off a sense of claustrophobia. Night shifts were rare for me—I usually worked earlier. A ringing in my ears matched the sound of a fluorescent light that flickered overhead. It was about to burn out completely.

I felt dulled by long hours inside the hospital. Since the shooting in Ballard, Annie was spooked with anxiety and had a doctor's order for light duty. Now, she only did assessments in controlled settings like these. To me, what happened that night was like being thrown from a horse; I had to get back to working in the field right away or I'd always be afraid.

According to Shandra, Laurel James had been found earlier that evening in the shower of a stranger's dormitory room at Seattle University, half-naked and covered in blood. When the student who lived there discovered her, Laurel ran outside into the late October cold. Finally, the Campus security caught up with her, wrapped her in a blanket and called an ambulance to take her to Harborview.

I glanced at the paperwork and learned that Ms. James was a 21-year-old student who had been hospitalized once before in the spring. My job was to determine if she fit one of Washington State's criteria for involuntary detention to a psychiatric unit. The possible options included danger to property, danger to self, danger to others, or grave disability. This meant that she was unable to meet her basic needs. Despite what we see on television, violent acts aren't usually committed by people with mental illness. They are more likely to be victims.

Shandra and I turned toward the doctor/parent standoff, but a voice from the television alcove called out, "Hey, I remember you." Two men in hospital pajamas congregated around the screen. One, a Russian who looked like a young Baryshnikov—deep-set eyes and a muscled physique that strained the one-size-fits-all pajama shirt—came up and gave me a fist bump. I would never forget him either. The last time I'd seen Victor was when I testified in court at the end of his 72-hour hold. He had been in a wheelchair with a waist and ankle restraint to keep him from fleeing while he was off the locked unit. When the assigned staff person unshackled Victor to use the bathroom, he entered the men's room, but returned naked moments later. "It's how we protest in Russia!" he claimed cheerfully. No security guard was in sight, so I'd helped talk him back into the wheelchair and get tethered again, all the while trying not to get too close to his youthful bareness.

Today, he asked, "You remember the Russian protest?" and ripped open the snaps on the green-striped top. In my career I'd seen more naked people than I wanted to.

I smiled but put my hand out to say stop. "Not again, please." He was on my list to evaluate too.

"It's been a long night," Shandra said and waved at the social worker's evaluation still clutched in my hand. The strobe-like light flickering above us made her movements seem jerky. "Now if you could get Mom to the family waiting area…"

Inside the tiny space, the woman moved to arrange her daughter's gown more modestly while the very young doctors tried to back her out of the room by talking and standing way too close.

My first impression had been like a snapshot. The young woman still hummed frantic nursery rhymes and leaned away from the commotion. Her honey-colored curls had dampened the blue hospital gown. Her arms were striped with razor cuts. Pinkish stains showed where water and blood had mixed, then dried while she was waiting to be evaluated. Eye makeup streaked down her face. She had a dimpled plumpness, maybe because she was on Olanzapine. One of its side effects was weight gain. She stared at the doctors with the darkest, most serious eyes I'd ever seen.

The mother and the doctors still crowded and argued, seemingly unaware of their effect on Laurel. The mother didn't give an inch. Her hair had fashionable dark roots and her lips and brows were made-up in heavy strokes. The embroidered name on her white jacket said "Mo," but in my quick scan I thought it said "Mom." Her shape was solid, but not heavy and reminded me of the round-shouldered refrigerator from the fifties that still purred in the Seattle kitchen of my mom's empty house. Mothers were on my mind.

I found her name on the paperwork. "Maureen James?" I said and put a gentle hand on her shoulder, introducing myself as the mental health evaluator who would be assessing her daughter for involuntary hospitalization. "Could I ask you a few questions?"

Maybe I was the first person who tried to talk rather than send her away, but she didn't hesitate to turn from the doctors to shake my hand. "Call me Mo." She looked familiar, but I didn't know why. I wondered if Laurel would look more like her as she aged.

"The doctors need to check Laurel's lacerations now. Could you come out to give me some history of her illness while we're waiting?" I wouldn't necessarily commit the daughter for cutting—it had become a sadly common way for young people to manage intense feelings. Often enough, the cuts were superficial, and hospitalization wasn't helpful, but from the picture I'd gotten, Laurel seemed seriously ill.

The family waiting room was off the secure unit. Mo James and I waited for someone to unlock the door, then I led her across the hall to another white and windowless room, this one furnished with a couch and armchair. She talked on the way; her words driven by worry. "I brought her to the Emergency Room yesterday, but they sent her home—how does this system help people? I try to keep her safe, but I have to sleep sometime." Mo James stiffly lowered herself into the chair. "Laurel didn't sleep, though. That's when she disappeared. I was looking everywhere when I finally got a call from Harborview."

I said how sorry I was for the inadequacies of the system, then explained the Involuntary Treatment Act. She was familiar with it already. "Early in their illness," I told her, "people often don't believe they need treatment."

Mo James shook her platinum head. "That's not Laurel. She takes medications, goes to a therapist, and reads everything she can find on how to manage. She's magnificent."

"Has she been under stress?" I asked, moved by the mother's ability to see her disheveled daughter as magnificent, all the while noticing that she didn't let in the awareness that her daughter had not agreed to treatment either day.

"She was at Stanford studying premed last year." Mo's words were fast with worry. "Then came the first hospitalization. I talked her into transferring to a school close to home. People in the hospital always ask if there is mental illness in the family. God knows both her father's family and mine are peculiar, but nothing diagnosable. Well, her father was a heroin addict, but I left him, and Laurel didn't grow up around that chaos. My family..." She shrugged and didn't describe them. "Laurel just saw this as a change of plans. She gave up med school and decided that she'd be a writer instead. She writes about her mental illness. But that led to her getting way too focused on it."

"How?" I asked.

"For therapy. She wrote reams." Her mother gave me the therapist's name.

I nodded. The behavior didn't set off any alarms. I'd evaluated people with notebooks full of tightly spaced words written in the throes of illness.

Mo smoothed her white jacket and tugged at a skirt which showed a lot of muscular leg.

"She spent all her time psychoanalyzing herself."

When I left Mo James in the Family Waiting Room to do my assessment, she begged me to hospitalize her daughter this time, but my interview would have to determine that.

Back in the PES, Laurel's arms and even her hands had been tidily dressed in gauze. Her dark blonde hair combed. She sat upright on the gurney. Now that the conflict between the doctors and her mother had been diverted, she seemed more settled, but her lips moved in a silent conversation. Still, she was able to focus when I introduced myself and explained her rights with the Miranda Warning.

"My first symptoms came when I was sixteen. Most people get their drivers licenses," she said with a warmth that drew me in. "I got psychotic."

This was an improvement from the blood stained, nursery-rhyming young woman I'd seen half an hour ago, but she was still preoccupied.

"I thought it was spiritual warfare. Demons came out of my bedroom ceiling," she continued and looked at me with horror in her eyes. "With tails and horns and stinking black fur. My job was to protect the world. I never told anyone though—I knew what was normal and what wasn't."

So, she had wrestled those demons by herself. I saw the magnificent side her mother mentioned—she had managed her delusions on her own back then. Sometimes delusions were fixed and telling someone there were no demons was impossible. Reality testing was the piece many people missed at the height of their illness. Laurel knew what was real, but I wondered how much that helped her.

"Are there demons here now?" I asked.

She gave a little smile. "Metaphoric demons. Plenty of those."

I smiled back, appreciating her wit. I really liked this young woman, but I remained silent to see if she would say anything else.

Finally, she continued. "They, the demons, were here. I knew I was getting crazy yesterday, but I already had an appointment with my therapist scheduled. My mom was there too. When I left, a demon followed." Laurel turned to examine the wall behind her as she talked. "I know that wasn't real."

She was calm, but I didn't believe the demons were all gone. Whatever it was, had led Laurel to cut herself in a stranger's shower after leaving her appointment. That wasn't over for her yet.

I explained the evaluation process and asked if she would agree to hospitalization.

She had turned back toward me. "I want help, but not the hospital. I can handle it at home."

Laurel's mental status might clear quickly. A medication adjustment and learning how to slow down in therapy would be in order. Given her behavior though, she wasn't safe in the community. I wrote and served the order to detain Laurel on a 72-hour hold. Establishing the legal grounds to hold her was simple: danger to self because she had cut her wrists and grave disability because she had not been thinking clearly enough to care for herself. Nothing pointed to danger to others.

The drive between home and the city had passed quickly while I played the scenes of Laurel and her mother over and over. Even with my preoccupation, I found rare on-street parking right by Harborview, Seattle's large regional trauma center.

Chapter 2

Annie had asked me to meet her in the fourth-floor meditation room. I didn't know such a place existed, much less how to find it. A volunteer with a book cart pointed me to the west sky bridge, a long hallway with windows on one side and offices on the other. I recognized it right away—stained glass in green and blue ripples bordered the door. Inside, an alcove held rolled prayer rugs. The main decor was Zen-like with wooden slats covering the wall in waves, but a red panic button chased my alpha state away. My training taught me to view small spaces with an eye on how to get out. These days, I was hyperaware. The only people here were two women in scrubs relaxing in upholstered chairs—and Annie, dressed in a soft brown shirt over narrow pants. She was in her element. Her fight or flight response quieted. No one even looked up when I entered.

Annie and I met in grad school in our twenties when we both wanted to be therapists. In our idealism, we thought we could heal people's pain. My own life was hectic then. Frank and I lived in a cluttered apartment and juggled work, school, and childcare for a toddling Nell. Annie, in counterpoint, lived in a Spartan apartment on Capitol Hill. I visited weekly for a quiet moment to study and chat. Annie's place was a needed refuge. I used to tease her about her monastic life, but I was closer to the truth than I realized at the time.

I touched Annie's arm and her eyes flew open. Her most striking feature was her pallor. Colorless lashes fringed her light blue eyes. Her hair looked like corn silk and fell past her shoulders. She got up silently and directed me to the hallway and the cushioned benches lining the wall of windows along the sky bridge.

"I'm worried about Laurel," Annie whispered.

"It's LJ." I said, using her initials because we were in a public space. "What happened?"

Annie's eyes fluttered as if she was having a hard time surfacing from her meditation. After grad school, she started out working with adolescents, changed to hospital social work, and finally landed in the Crisis and Commitment Office. We'd both worked there for the past ten years. I loved evenings when we partnered in the field, driving to every edge of the county doing evaluations and talking all the way. After the Cole shooting, things changed. Annie told me that in her career, she never had felt she could help people. Now she just wanted to pray for them. I should have seen it coming. Annie was already studying at Seattle University's school of Theology and Ministry. After the shooting, she entered the Chaplaincy Program. She wanted a job change and the sooner the better. That's how she met Laurel—as part of her internship to become a hospital chaplain.

Everything in Annie's life had shifted—to before the shooting and after the shooting. After, I saw less of Annie. She no longer worked in the field; school took up her free time. Soon she would leave our team for good. With Gwen in France and Nell on her their way there, I couldn't help feeling abandoned.

That day in Ballard left other marks. Nate Fischer, the police officer recovered and went back to work. Calvin Cole survived but wasn't so lucky. I'd heard that he might be in a wheelchair for life. Annie still lived with the aftereffects; a door slamming, in fact any loud noise sent her into panic. Slowly she was getting back to her old calm and centered self.

We sat with our knees pointing toward each other on one of the cushioned benches that lined the sky bridge windows. "Everything was usual," she told me when I asked about her meeting with Laurel. Few chaplains had Annie's experience with people in the psychiatric units, she was the star intern. "I asked Laurel about any faith tradition she has, what helps. She wanted me to pray with her."

I nodded.

"Then she told me how fortunate she was to understand her illness more than most people. That she had her therapist to help her sort out reality." Annie's foot tapped against the boxy window seat, speeding up, a hollow beat like a pulse. "I was pretty sure she was telling me what she thought I wanted to hear. I could see her struggling. Finally, she blurted it out—she thought her therapist had become a demon. That's when Laurel said she'd killed her."

"I'm going to talk to her. I'll meet you later." I said, still thinking about Laurel's demons. I remembered her covered in blood and hoped it was her own. I wanted to revisit my assessment—had Laurel pulled my heartstrings too much? Mostly, I wanted to protect Annie's tentative comeback from the shooting trauma.

Harborview's three psychiatric units were housed on the fifth floor. Laurel was in unit 5MB, or psychiatric intensive care. I'd originally thought she would be a better fit on a unit with groups and more freedom. Before my job with Crisis and Commitment, I'd been a social worker on 5MB. Visiting a patient I'd detained was irregular at best, but I still had friends working on the unit and figured I could slip in a visit to Laurel if I showed up with donuts. I headed down Ninth Avenue to the Stockbox grocery and waited in a ten-minute line to pick up pastries for the staff and two lattes, one with lots of caffeine to keep me awake and one decaf for Laurel because I didn't want to create more anxiety. Then I headed back to the hospital and took the elevators and sky bridges and entered a little alcove with a wall mounted telephone outside the locked door. I balanced both cups on my pastry box to make the call. I had to know if my first assessment was a mistake.

Crystal, a heavy-set blonde in blue scrubs met me and led me through the first set of locked doors, eyeing the cardboard container with delight. I told her I was the evaluator who had written the commitment papers on Laurel.

"I thought she'd be on a less restrictive unit," I said.

"Maybe you don't know then."

"Know what?"

"She tried to follow the housekeeper out the door in the PES.

And *voila*. Now she is on 5MB where it is much harder to elope." Crystal used the terminology for what the rest of the world would call escape. She led to the second locked door.

"Laurel didn't want to be in the hospital." I remarked. Most people didn't, but I wondered about Laurel's drive to leave.

The nurse led me onto the unit where a wall-mounted television blared a reality show. To my right, a dining table with swivel chairs attached always reminded me of playground equipment. It was really intended to prevent anyone throwing the furniture.

Laurel came out of a patient room down the hall. Perfect timing. I passed the donuts to Crystal and tilted my head in the young woman's direction. "I hate to admit it, but I brought her a latte."

"You softy," she said. "Go on, I'll talk to you later."

Tidy bandages covered Laurel's arms and hands. Too tight striped pants showed some weight gain. Her honey-colored hair was pulled back and long bangs framed her face. She looked more like her mother than she had the night before. She didn't wear the dramatic makeup, but she had the naturally heavy brows minus the make-up. Her serious eyes brightened a little when I handed her the coffee.

We found a sort-of private table in a corner and slid into the attached seats. I explained that I was here to visit the staff and hoped to see how she was. In truth, she looked like she was doing well. The question I really wanted to ask—*did you kill your therapist*—was the one likely to bring the least information, so I talked informally to establish trust. After we discussed hospital food, I said, "I can tell you take care of yourself. What are you working on in your therapy sessions? Sometimes people want to work hard but going too fast can cause problems."

"I know," she said. "That's what my therapist said."

So, Laurel's mental state had concerned her therapist too. Emotions played over the young woman's face. First, she looked like she'd said too much, then too little. "I do cognitive work with my symptoms, but we also work on relationships. Fathers to be specific. I'm getting to know my dad. My parents divorced when I was four."

"Is he local?"

"He lives in California, but he's a musician up here performing with friends. I have a month with him."

"How's that going?" I asked. "Your mom said she'd cut off contact with him because of addiction."

"He's clean and sober now, and so much warmer than my mom. She's too involved with work and micromanaging my life."

I smiled and told her my daughter might describe me the same way.

Laurel wrapped her gauze covered arms around herself and looked conflicted as she talked about her parents. "Jimmy—my dad—is into 12-steps. He helps me understand my recovery too. Mom doesn't know he's here yet. She cut off all contact. That's not the best model for learning about relationships."

I nodded, remembering that her mother's experience had been before the 12-step stage.

"She still won't budge," Laurel said as if she knew what I was thinking. She picked at the white tape that secured the dressing on her fingers and looked around the shabby room where a previous patient had made pencil drawings on the wall. "Sometimes we have to protect our parents from the hard stuff."

I raised my eyebrows.

"I know. My therapist made the same face. She told me to be careful, but my dad is only here for a month. I don't have time for that."

That was the second time she compared me to her therapist which made me a little nervous. I thought that general talk about her therapy might shake something out about murder but hadn't gotten that. I decided to approach from a different direction. "Are you still bothered by demons?"

Laurel considered her paper cup. She had only taken a few sips and the milk had already started to separate from the coffee. "I may always be bothered by demons. It's how I manage them that counts."

Her answer sounded pat. She was smart and knew how to talk to professionals. This answer was skating on the surface. Now I'd see if my relationship building paid off when I asked more pointed questions. "The nurse told me you tried to follow someone out the door when you were downstairs. Where were you planning to go?"

"I have to find…" Laurel shook her head as if to clear it, but she couldn't finish the sentence.

I gave her plenty of time to answer, but her eyes had an anxious look now. I knew she was stuck. "I'm worried, Laurel. You told the chaplain that you killed your therapist."

Her mouth still held a partially formed word that didn't come out. After a minute, she said, "I love my therapist." She hadn't responded to what I'd said.

"Did you kill her?" I said it without judgement.

Finally, Laurel's voice became a whisper. "I don't know. She was following me home and she wasn't the same person."

I waited.

"It was dark." Laurel sat a long time before the next words came out. "It sounds crazy."

"I'm just trying to find out what happened."

"Her face changed. Her clothes changed. I turned on Broadway to get away." She looked at her bandaged hand and rubbed it in a way that was sure to hurt. "She got to my apartment before me. I don't remember. Leaning on the dumpsters. Red, blue, green."

"Laurel," I said gently, "Take a breath." I inhaled and blew it out slowly, partly to have her follow my example, partly to keep myself present too.

Her breath mirrored mine and she looked up like she was searching. "I thought she was a demon. Is she dead?"

"I don't know," I said and realized that in my rush to leave my mother's makeshift memorial and meet Annie, I'd never checked.

On my way out, I stopped into the busy nursing station. Laurel's social worker, Joe Marston, a fuzzy-looking man who was probably five inches shorter than me, stood brushing powdered sugar from his burgundy sweater in the cramped alcove behind the main work area. The box of donuts was empty except for one half of something filled with red goo. Joe had come on staff after I left the hospital, but we talked from time to time.

"Thanks for the donuts," he said.

"My pleasure. Laurel James looks pretty good. I was wondering if you'd been able to contact her therapist."

He studied his sweater and removed a final crumb. "I left a message but haven't heard back."

Chapter 3

The therapist's name was Marion Warfield. I put in my own call on the way to meet Annie in the cramped chaplains' office in the hospital basement. I left a voicemail, but by this time, I had a bad feeling and wasn't expecting a call back. Annie sat at a long green Formica desk typing notes from her last visit.

"What did you say in Laurel's note," I asked.

"I haven't written it yet." Annie brushed a strand of fine hair out of her face. She raised her shoulders lightly and looked more stuck than stubborn. "That's why I called you. I want to show she's innocent before I turn it in."

"Oh Annie, I don't think that's possible." I hadn't realized Laurel's story had hit her that hard and couldn't help but wonder if she needed more of a career change than the Chaplaincy was going to give her.

"We don't know if the therapist is dead," she said.

"Right, but we have to finish all the reports before we leave tonight. With whatever we do know." I said even though my eyes were starting to feel gluey from not enough sleep. I needed to talk to my supervisor, Vera March, to sort out what to do about this possible homicide. But first, I could give in to Annie just a little. I waved a Post It Note where I'd scribbled Laurel's address before leaving the psych unit. "Her apartment is close. Let's check it out. I want to walk where Laurel had walked, get a feeling for what happened. Along the way, we'll figure out the rest. Are you coming?"

There was no window in the room to gage the amount of daylight left. "It's late," she said, looking at her watch. "Four o'clock."

21

"Sunset is at six. I'm not going alone." I smiled to myself, wishing this was one step to getting Annie back into the field, for a little while at least.

"Alright," she said and picked up her coat.

Laurel's apartment, on 13th and Jefferson, was five blocks from Harborview. Seattle's growth spree was visible everywhere. To the right, Yesler Terrace, once low-slung housing for World War II workers and later low-income housing, was now a pit in the ground, soon to be condominiums. Late afternoon traffic was building, and the sidewalks were in shadow. The street trees glimmered against the perfect fall sky, but clear skies brought cold temperatures. I wished for my gloves that had been packed away since last winter. I couldn't untangle my thoughts. The holes in the ground reminded me of the memorial that morning and I wondered if we should have had Mom buried instead of cremated—something more substantial.

We turned onto Jefferson and came across another block-long hole. Annie and I stopped and watched the excavation in silence. I felt as if we were losing the city and struggled to remember what had been there: a 1950s apartment building where a Somali nurse I knew had lived, a Victorian house converted to a lawyer's office, a parking lot. Heavy equipment scraped and loaded the earth into trucks that hauled it away. Their vibrations made the sidewalk tremble beneath our feet.

"We scattered Mom's ashes this morning." I said and struggled to find words to tell Annie about the emptiness.

She put an arm around my shoulders. "You should have told me. I would have come."

Her warmth confused me. "You know I'm not religious."

Annie sighed. Her pale skin was pink with the cool air and looked more ethereal than ever. "It doesn't have to be religious. People need ceremony. I'd have brought you Rumi poems. Secular Seattle loves Rumi."

"I know," I said. At times like this, I wished I had faith like Annie's. I stopped going to church as soon as my mother and grandmother allowed it. Organized religion never took hold with me. I'd rather work in the garden. "Anyway, Nell took over." I explained the ritual she'd made but didn't discuss my ambivalence. "The pancakes were pretty good."

Annie smiled sadly. We had talked about our families over the years. She knew about my mother's struggle with depression. It was no surprise that I became a social worker, maybe to save Mom, more likely to save myself.

We left the construction site and walked toward Seattle University, a Jesuit run school where Annie reveled in daily Mass and studied for her career change. From here, we followed the path Laurel had likely taken from her therapist's office at the university to her apartment. The trees and gardens on the city campus glowed with autumn color, but Laurel had an evening appointment. It would have been dark for her.

We passed the ballfield on the corner of 12th and James. Turning there like Laurel had would lead away from her apartment on 13th and Jefferson. Annie and I took the direct route and found her address, an old brick apartment with a Tudor facade and street-level storefronts. Painted advertisements from the 1930s had faded on the dark brick. In the current market it was probably destined to be another hole in the ground soon.

"What are we looking for?" I asked, realizing that like this morning, I had come without a plan.

"We'll find out," Annie said.

I stepped forward and she followed me around the corner—it was exactly as Laurel had described. I saw the row of dumpsters in different colors. Red, blue, green. But no yellow tape. I tried to see it from Laurel's point of view.

A doll-like young woman in a black lace dress and boots came out of a storefront. Her dyed-black hair set off a light complexion. She propped the door and carried out a bucket and broom. She was just about to dump soapy water on the sidewalk when I realized why and hurried over.

"Wait."

Her purpose was clear, blood, now the color of rust, had pooled and dried on the sidewalk. There really had been a stabbing. Here.

The Goth girl shook her head in distress. "I thought the city would send someone to clean up, but no one came. I wasn't sure if it was okay for me to do it, you know, maybe the police needed something. I called to ask, but never got a response. I manage this building. I have a business to run. My customers don't mind creepy—but I don't want to scare them away."

A sandwich sign on the sidewalk advertised custom built caskets. I glanced at the storefront; gold leaf framed the display windows and advertised *Curiosities and Haunted Goods*. A hanging noose swung in one window, the other staged a scene from Little Red Riding Hood with a caped mannequin and a taxidermy wolf. More preserved animals looked on, a squirrel, a badger, all once living, now moth-eaten. A still-shiny black crow looked over the eerie tableau with an inscrutable beaked face. Under normal circumstances, I would be amused by the scene, but today, flirtation with death culture seemed a sad irony.

Annie, on the other hand, took to the young woman right away. She touched her arm, "I'm so sorry. This is where the stabbing happened." She said it as a statement, not a question.

"How did you know?" The young woman's eyes teared up.

"I'm a Chaplain at Harborview and heard about it there. That's why I came." Annie knelt and touched the rusty looking blood. The shopkeeper followed suit. Together they studied the stain. "When I was a girl," Annie said, "I was out with my aunt. A car ran off the road and hit her. It looked like this, but the blood was fresh. She died in my arms."

Annie's story was what this young woman needed. They perched together on the edge of the bloodstain for so long I fought off the urge to pick up the bucket of soapy water and clean everything myself. I'd had all the emotion I could tolerate for one day. Cleaning seemed like the best therapy. I looked longingly at the bucket but let them talk. Instead, I would dig into what happened. I pulled out my phone and checked the Seattle Police Department blog to see if there was any report of the stabbing. I cringed when I read: *Info sought on 13th Ave Capitol Hill Stabbing. Vic unknown.*

Vic. Even though I understood the need for abbreviation in Twitter length messages, I hated the dehumanizing word. The message didn't say if the victim was dead or alive. From the amount of blood, I thought I knew.

I realized Nate might be able to get some information and texted him. We'd become friends during his long, slow recovery from the shooting at the Cole house. The situation seemed too much to explain in a text, so I just asked him to call me about what I'd seen. When I finished, I tucked my phone into my pocket.

"Do you know what happened?" Annie asked.

"I don't." The doll-like woman answered in a string of halting phrases. "I heard sirens and looked out to a sea of flashing lights. It wasn't raining. Rain would have washed this. Earlier, I'd been in the shop and heard a noise. A woman's voice. A whoop or a moan. It's haunting me. If only I'd checked the moment I heard."

I looked at the blood on the ground but asked just to confirm it. "Did she die?"

"I came out when I heard the sirens. The ambulance drivers said she'd probably died damn fast."

"Did you hear her name?"

She shook her head.

Annie looked drawn; her skin had lost its pink in the time the two crouched, talking on the sullied concrete. I knew she still carried all the trauma she'd experienced starting with her aunt's death when she was so young. It was heavy. No wonder she didn't bounce back from Nate's shooting. The young woman sensed it too and put her arm out to steady her.

Finally, the two stood up and Annie pulled out her card. "Please, call me if you want to talk."

As we walked away, the young woman tipped the bucket of soapy water onto the blood-stained sidewalk and began to sweep. *A tisket, a tasket, I really need a casket*—Laurel's rhyme in the PES took on new meaning. She lived above a casket store and there had been a terrible stabbing here.

Chapter 4

Annie and I walked back to the old art deco entrance of the hospital without talking and headed to the Chaplain's Office. Fortunately, we had the narrow room to ourselves. While Annie typed the note describing her talk with Laurel, I called our supervisor at the Crisis and Commitment office. Vera and I went over the legal implications of Laurel's confession and agreed that I'd submit a statement to the police.

"I don't think Laurel did it," Annie said so Vera could hear. She looked like she was watching a bad movie in her head. "She shouldn't get stuck on the forensics unit at Western State Hospital."

After the call, I tried to get back to my typing, but Annie was still thinking about Laurel and Western. She pointed to my report. "We have to prove it wasn't Laurel. Something like half of all murders go unsolved. The police will be thrilled to have someone like Laurel to take in. Someone with mental illness."

I felt the tug of working together with Annie one more time and said okay. Then I submitted my documentation, with a copy to Joe Marston on the unit.

Annie rested her forehead on her palm.

"Hey, are you alright?" I spoke. "Do you want to go out for a drink? Or tea. Whatever?"

She came back to herself and responded. "I'm fine, Grace. I just need some time. I'll see you at work tomorrow."

"Okay," I gave her a hug good-bye. Her body was tight.

Now I wanted to see what Joe Marston thought. As Laurel's social worker he might have more insight into what had happened.

I should have talked to him when I was on the unit, but in my way, I had been trying to protect Annie. On my way out of the basement office, I realized that my timing was terrible. All the social workers had gone home for the day. I could only leave him a message with what I'd learned and tell him I'd talk to him tomorrow. A rush hour commute was next, with a million cars idled on the freeway just below the hospital. I got in the Prius and turned on the news, prepared to inch toward I-90, the floating bridge across Lake Washington. Brake lights glowed red like a string of beads across the water and didn't thin out even after I passed Novelty Hill.

NPR switched from *All Things Considered* to local news with a report on an upcoming court case related to the police shooting a mentally ill man last year. I clenched the steering wheel when I realized that it was my personal experience of a police shooting. Calvin Cole's parents were suing the hospital that evaluated him the day before we were called to the house. The case was based on the failure to safely hospitalize him when he was so ill that he shot a policeman. "Our son regrets his actions. He shot a policeman, true, but he suffers from a mental disorder." The mother went on about the trauma he had suffered. That day had brought trauma to us all—and the court case would keep it alive. I wished her well. Since he was in a wheelchair, Calvin might need expensive care. The newscaster moved on, but I remembered the media storm that the shooting had originally caused; I turned the radio off.

Our house was ten minutes the other side of Duvall. The sky held the deep blue that comes just before full darkness. From Mountain View Road, I pulled up our driveway and left the car in front of what would have been a double garage but served as storage for cords of firewood and a workshop for Frank. The sound of gravel under my tires alerted Caesar. The husky ran to greet me with a glint in his eyes and spun in circles in his excitement. The whine of a skill saw told me Frank was still working on some repair.

Frank finished his cut and brushed a layer of sawdust from his down vest before I kissed him hello. The sharpness of freshly cut cedar smelled clean. I was glad to be home.

"How are you holding up?" he asked.

"Exhausted. Hungry," I said and asked what he was working on.

"The pump house door is full of rot. I noticed it when we were down at the creek with Rose's ashes."

We both knew the pump house door had been falling off its hinges and impossible to open for years. Maybe this was Frank's way of fixing things up for Mom's resting place. "I want to get down there and clear out the path for her." I said as if she could appreciate the improvements. The book on grief would probably recommend it.

Frank said he'd shut shop for the day and we planned for dinner—omelets, quick and easy. I walked back to the chicken house to gather the eggs I'd neglected in the morning. I opened the laying box and pulled out my sweater to make a cradle and filled it with enough green and brown eggs to tell me I hadn't collected them yesterday either. My phone vibrated in my pocket. I arranged the clutch of eggs to keep them safe and secured the coop for the night. By the time I reached for the phone, I'd missed the call. The screen said it was Nate Fisher.

I remembered when Nate had been in the hospital for a week after Calvin Cole put a bullet in his shoulder. I visited him on my way to work every afternoon. I was drawn to sit with him after the shooting—as if I could will him to heal by being there. Annie would have called it prayer.

The first time I went, another officer sat beside him. I'd heard that the police department does this after a shooting and marveled at how they support their injured. I knew then that I needed to spend more time with Annie. We had received a flurry of concern from our coworkers, but we weren't physically injured. At times, the questions they asked about what happened and what we could have done differently felt critical. I couldn't tell if others blamed me or if I was blaming myself.

That day, the officer with Nate stepped out for coffee so we could talk. Nate was too big for the bed. His feet touched the bottom rail. He looked like a tank under the sheet, and I wondered what nicknames he'd had as a child. Tubes and drains gurgled with fluids. He kept his hair in a crew cut, a look I thought of as military, but with his grinning good nature he never seemed intimidating. Now, his face pinched with pain, he clicked the morphine pump and asked me to sit down.

"I like the company, but I hope you don't mind if I doze," he said. So, he drifted in and out and I pretended to read for an hour.

The next time I visited, he was more alert. Not knowing what to say, I gave the standard "I've been thinking of you."

His big, expressive face broke into a full-on smile. "I'll bet you have," he said. "Every night, just when you're about to fall asleep, you jerk awake and see me fall again."

"Something like that." I couldn't deny it. "Actually, exactly like that. You too?" We discussed our heightened startle reflexes and dreams, and I felt better, like we were in this together and would get out of it too.

The memory made me smile. I returned his call on my way into the house.

"Hi, Nate."

"You heard the news?"

"The Cole lawsuit, yep." I reached for a bowl from the shelves by the back door to unload the eggs. Then I grabbed an open bottle of Cabernet, poured a glass, and sank into a chair at the kitchen table.

"Are we going to be subpoenaed?" he asked. "They're saying he should have been detained before we ever saw him."

"The attorneys have already requested the records. I know he'd been evaluated before, but I can't remember any details without reading the paperwork." I took a sip of wine and tried to relax. "That's not even why I called. I saw on the SPD blog that there was a stabbing on Capitol Hill. 13th and Jefferson. Do you know anything about it?"

A guttural sound came across the line. "I was the officer who took the call. Bad. Very bloody."

"I evaluated a young woman who was talking about it. It sounded like she saw something, but I couldn't tell what was real and what wasn't. Annie and I went up there and saw where the blood had dried." As if it would protect Laurel, I didn't tell him yet about Laurel's confession even though I'd sent the police report.

"That's going above and beyond," he said. "So, what did the woman you evaluated say?"

"Well, she *is* psychotic. She said the woman was a demon."

Frank had already washed up and pulled a bunch of vegetables out of the refrigerator waving them at me to ask how he should proceed with dinner. I mouthed "Can you do it?" and took the phone and my wine out to the back porch to finish the call.

"Sounds crazy, but she got that right," Nate said. "You should have seen her. Ripped black lace and shit. Overly made up. Looked like something out of a Chucky movie. Her eyes were black with make-up. I hope she was going clubbing."

It sounded too much like what Laurel had said to be coincidence, but it didn't sound like a therapist who had just left a session with a troubled student.

"Her hair was dark blonde and totally teased," he continued.

"The blog said the victim was unknown."

"You don't expect us to report everything, do you? Her name was Marion Warfield."

I winced to hear it. Everything looked bad for Laurel.

"We found her handbag," he went on. "The wallet and phone had been taken, but there was other stuff. Could have been a robbery gone bad, but it felt too violent for that."

"What else was there?" I wanted to know more about what I had seen in the aftermath.

"Like I said, it was bad. She'd been cut from ear to ear. There was blood everywhere." He paused, probably remembering. "She must have died in a minute. Some guy really did her in."

I groaned at the image, but his assumption that the murderer was a man stopped me. Laurel wasn't more than five foot three. "How about a woman? Could a woman have killed her?"

"Women don't usually do the violent crimes. There's always a chance, though."

Nate had described blood everywhere. By the time I saw her,

the blood on Laurel looked reasonable given her lacerations, but she was wearing hospital clothes, and she had already been in the stranger's shower.

"Nate, this woman, she told Annie she killed her therapist."

"Whose name is Marion Warfield? Who turned up dressed like a demon?"

"Right. When I talked to her, she seemed unsure, confused. Her delusions were about demons, but then she sees her therapist like that and right in front of her apartment. I just filed my report. What do you think the police will do?"

"It's a murder investigation, Grace. You know what they'll do. Try to make a case and bring someone in."

I thanked Nate; glad I'd be back to Seattle first thing tomorrow to talk to the staff on the unit about Laurel's confession.

The chill air turned to mist on the field and yellow light from the windows made the garden eerie with black shapes. Nell's cottage was dark. She was spending almost every evening with friends before she left on her trip. I looked at my wine glass, surprised I'd emptied it already, and went inside to help with dinner.

Frank had already washed the salad greens. I took over that task because he could flip the best omelet. I had a lot to tell. While I ripped lettuce and sliced avocado, I caught him up on everything from blood on the sidewalk to Annie's reactions and my need to go into the city early tomorrow. Then I poured more wine and we sat down to eat the buttery omelets. I finally ran out of news.

Frank ate for a few minutes then paused and cleared his throat. "You're doing it again Grace."

I froze with my fork halfway to my mouth. "What?" But I knew.

"You are getting over-involved with the young woman you evaluated."

There was truth enough in what he said. Something about Laurel made me want to mother her.

"It's like when Martin was killed," Frank kept going. Our

neighbor and two other men had been murdered a few years ago. A young woman I'd evaluated helped me find the killer. But this was different.

"It's Annie. She's worried about this girl and she's not coping." I ticked off the layers of her ordeals while avoiding my own: how seeing her aunt die made her more vulnerable and she was still anxious after Calvin Cole's shooting.

"I'd say you have as much stress as Annie." Frank counted the murders on his fingers, adding my mother's death and Nell's leaving.

I swirled what was left in my glass and studied the rich red wine—then finished it and reached for more. A sure sign that Frank was hitting home. I didn't care. "Some years are just shitty, but I'm more worried about Annie than myself."

"Just wondering why you're bringing more trouble into your life when you could just as easily encourage Annie to let it go."

"Thanks," I said. Because I didn't have an answer, I got up to wash the dishes. The activity didn't calm my thoughts, though. A therapist dressed as a demon, following a client home. It made no sense. As soon as I'd finished my chore, I went to my desk and turned on the laptop. When I typed in Marion Warfield's name, I was surprised to see so many citations. Most therapists kept a low profile online, not wanting clients to become over-involved with web searches.

Not Marion Warfield. She was everywhere. She had a master's degree in Counseling and a PhD in Divinity. She had written a book called *The Other Deepest Thing* and had a weekly radio show about spirituality on NPR. Even though I had never heard of her, Laurel's therapist was apparently rather famous. When the police finally released her name, the media would be all over it. Now I was glad they were keeping it quiet. In her pictures, I saw the dark blonde hair, tousled and curling on her shoulders. Her deep-set eyes looked warm and intelligent. A younger Meryl Streep might have been cast to play her. She looked like she was in her late thirties, with a calmness in her expression. I would trust her.

"I can't imagine the fishnet stockings." I said to myself and texted a copy of her photo to Nate saying, *Is this her?* His answer came right back. *Yes. But so different.* I tried to imagine her as a demon. Not just dressed up but burning inside.

Chapter 5

Annie's voice was thick and phlegmy when I called the next morning.

"What did you tell your chaplaincy supervisor about Laurel?" I asked.

"I just left a message and told him to read the note." she croaked. "I called in sick. I feel terrible. I'd never be able to do my internship this morning and then go to work until midnight."

As long as I'd known her, Annie had coped with stress by getting sick. She'd been preoccupied with Laurel James. Everything we learned made the young woman look worse. Annie had been traumatized in childhood—that changes a person. I remembered how the policeman had sat with Nate after he'd been shot.

I'd bring her soup.

Annie had lived in the same apartment on 15th Avenue East since grad school. The building, a 1930s walk-up with a cream-colored brick façade and large bay windows, was squeezed between two new glassy developments. There was no intercom. In the old days, I pitched pebbles at the window to get her attention. Now I phoned, and she tossed down the keys, so I could let myself in.

Annie's apartment was spare, but comfortable. No excess of books or clutter here, just large expanses of wood floors she'd sanded herself, oriental rugs and a few paintings that were well done, though a little too darkly religious for my taste. She sat, curled into an overstuffed chair by the bay windows. Annie's hair hung stringy and unwashed. Crumpled Kleenex littered the floor. To me, the room felt overheated, but she wrapped a quilt around her shoulders and still shivered. I'd picked up Pho Gà in cardboard containers at a Vietnamese restaurant on 12th and held up the bag with its separate containers of hot broth, noodles, and vegetables.

"Chicken soup," I said. "Do you want it now or should I put it in the fridge for later?"

She put her hands out to accept my offering. "Share it with me."

I went to the kitchen for bowls. The once sunny window was blocked by a glassy black building just a few feet away. I railed against overdevelopment, but Annie just put in a grow light and climbing plants to improve the outlook. I found two blue and white, dragon bowls in the cupboard and served the soup.

I pulled up a chair and listened while she detailed the symptoms of her cold. I was impatient with her and told her the news. "I talked to Nate."

"How is he?"

"Good."

Annie smiled and waited, so I went on. "He was the one who answered the call to the stabbing." If that is what you would call a slit throat. I left out his description of the blood. Annie and I had seen the stains the next day.

"Really." Annie's already bleary eyes filled with tears. "I don't usually tell you about my prayer life. This has really gotten to me. I've been praying about it."

"I know." I wanted to tell her what else I learned before she cut me off. "The woman was Laurel's therapist." I described her dress and how it looked as demon-like as Laurel had said. "We set out to prove that what Laurel said was caused by her illness, but it wasn't."

Annie took in the news silently at first, then spoke. "We've worked in this field for years, Grace. I can feel it in my gut when someone is a danger. So can you. Of course we have to collect evidence, but I just don't see Laurel as dangerous."

I would trust Annie's instincts any day. She could assess a situation in an instant, like the time she clutched my shoulder and moved me away just as a woman we were evaluating swung her closed fist. I felt the air move where my face had just been. "Unfortunately, facts aren't supporting your feelings."

Annie shook her head. "Did she set off any alarms for you, Grace?"

"No, but everything we learn points to her. Today, I'm going to talk to the social worker. Laurel's court date is tomorrow." To protect their rights, patients had a hearing to determine if they still presented enough risk to require hospitalization at the end of 72 hours. "I don't know what the police are going to do or when, but I have to make sure she's not released."

Annie responded by blowing her nose. For a few moments, we sipped our soup from white porcelain spoons in silence.

I gave her the rest of my news. "I looked up the therapist online. Her name is Marion Warfield. She seems to be a big name in spirituality."

Annie put her bowl on the side table and sat quietly, her ethereal skin more waxen now. The soup wasn't helping when the talk was about the problem.

"You know her?"

She closed her eyes. She looked stricken. "I've seen her at SU. That's all."

I stared at the patterns in the rug, dark blue flowers with tan spaces woven on a maroon background.

Finally, she spoke again. "I saw my doctor Monday—about my anxiety. She released me to full duty at work. I won't be doing just the in-hospital evaluations."

"That was before Laurel," I said. "You don't feel ready, do you?"

"At the time, I thought I felt as ready as I ever would."

"Why didn't you tell me?"

"I was too anxious." Annie adjusted her cocoon of blankets.

"Can't you get your doc to approve more light duty or time off if you need it?" I moved to sit on the arm of the chair and leaned down to hug her. She melted into the touch.

"Can't afford it," she said. "I'm out of leave time."

Before I left Annie's apartment, I made an appointment to meet Joe Marston, the social worker at 5MB. Then, I hoped to get downtown in time for my afternoon meeting. Like Annie, my gut told me that Laurel wasn't a killer, but everything we learned added confusion.

I parked three blocks from the hospital and walked west, squinting into the afternoon sun, past an old brick building under renovation. The builders had saved the street trees and I kicked at fallen leaves as I walked. From the corner, Harborview's blond brick façade and the matching healthcare buildings across the street framed Mount Rainier. I went in near the Emergency Department and waited for an always-slow-elevator with a group of new medical students who perked up their ears when an overhead announcement reported a Code Zebra and instructed all staff to check their email. The group argued over what a Code Zebra might mean and filled the entire elevator when it came. I waited. A second elevator finally arrived, and I smiled at a citrus scent that lingered from the last occupant. The hospital wasn't known for appealing smells. When I hit 5, a man with a bushy beard and dark, slicked-back hair ran to get on. I swung my bag to keep the doors open.

"What floor?" I asked. He wanted the fifth too.

The man peeled off his leather jacket revealing a muscled arm and an impressive sleeve tattoo that incorporated a musical staff, notes, and the initials JJ. On second glance, he seemed a little older than I'd thought, his hair threaded with white. He ignored elevator etiquette and talked all the way up. "Who knew it would be this sunny in Seattle. Are you from here?"

I nodded with a slight smile. Seattleites weren't chatty under any circumstances, much less in an enclosed space.

He didn't even notice and rambled on. "I've heard about the 5th floor—where you go if you're crazy. I didn't expect to know someone there, but my daughter... "She's going home today and asked me to pick her up." The doors slid open, and he stepped out and looked around, confused.

"There are three psychiatric units," I told him. "Which one are you looking for?"

He squinted at a scrap of paper. "5 Maleng Building?"

I pointed him to the right and paused to collect my thoughts before I headed to 5MB myself. Maybe Laurel would be as responsible for her treatment as her mother said and agree to stay in the hospital—unless the police showed up with a warrant.

I headed toward the unit. From the sky bridge, I looked south down 9th Avenue, past the old steam plant, the ubiquitous construction cranes, and the mountain again. The wall of windows was lined with chairs facing the view where staff took breaks and families clustered to discuss loved ones out of earshot.

At the far end, was an alcove with locked metal doors that lead to the psychiatric unit and a wall-mounted telephone where visitors phoned for admittance. I went around to Joe's social work office, but it was empty. He was probably on the unit. Laurel's mother and the man from the elevator were talking in the alcove. Their interaction seemed intense. I went back to the skybridge to give them a moment's privacy and pretended to focus on my phone screen like everyone else, but I could still see them from the corner of my eye.

Today, instead of a white chef's jacket, Mo James wore a red blazer as bright as her lipstick. The color made her look fashionable in a boxy way. I wondered if the man was Laurel's father and remembered that she hadn't told her mother he was in town or even that she was in touch with him. Mo stepped away from him as if she couldn't get enough distance in the small space. They seemed an improbable pair, Maureen James, professional with platinum hair and her ex, looking hip in a different way. I couldn't help but eavesdrop.

"Jimmy." Mo said it with a voice laced with coolness and maybe a little panic. "How did you get here?"

"I've been in touch with Laurel for a few months," he said. "It's nice to see you, Mo."

She didn't return the pleasantry. "I don't have the energy to bring you up-to-date. Laurel has been very ill." She picked up the wall phone to the unit and dialed in. "I'm calling again. I've been waiting here forever, and no one has come to let me in."

"Tell them I'm here too," he said.

Mo gave him a grudging look and spoke into the phone, then hung up the earpiece a little too hard when she finished. "Someone will be with us in a minute—as they said ten minutes ago."

Laurel's father took a step forward. "You don't have to do this on your own. I've been clean and sober for fifteen years. I can help."

"I can't trust you just because you say so. Trust is earned. You're the one who left Laurel at home alone when I was at work. You were supposed to be taking care of her. No." Her voice dripped with sarcasm. "Off to find drugs."

"I tried..." He started, then stopped himself letting the thought dangle. "What I did was my fault, but she's not a kid anymore. When you're ready, I hope I can make amends."

"She has enough problems without you." Mo said.

"Kids want to know their parents," he echoed what Laurel had said when I last saw her. I could tell they had been talking about this. "Don't forget, I'm the one who helped when you needed it most."

I wondered about the time when Mo needed him and decided it must have been long ago, then announced my presence and stepped into the alcove. The citrus perfume from the elevator clung to Mo and I felt sad that the cheery scent and all her good intentions didn't prevent this family strife.

I greeted them and explained my role to the father.

"Jimmy James," He introduced himself and took my hand. His eyes were dark and liquid, how I imagined Laurel's would look when she wasn't troubled.

Mo touched my arm and I felt like Laurel's whole family was clinging to me for support. I explained that I was here to speak to Laurel's social worker and made my own call to the office.

Two public safety officers badged onto the unit while we waited. Next the group of medical students came and huddled with their supervisor who explained that Code Zebra signified a missing patient. Mo glowered when someone came and asked her to wait just a little longer. She looked at her watch and said, "I have a meeting at 2:00. I want to have time to visit."

The door finally clicked open again and Joe Marston, in the same burgundy sweater he'd worn the day before, stepped into the cramped entryway. I frowned, thinking how upset the family would be if I too entered before they did, but Joe just nodded to me and spoke to the family instead. "I'm sorry you had to wait." He covered his mouth with his fist and cleared his throat, then glanced at Mo. "We can't find your daughter. She seems to have escaped."

The tiny alcove closed in.

Mo spoke first. "What happened? What can we do?" The impatience and irritability had left her voice. Maybe, like me, a sense of purpose helped her.

Joe cleared his throat again and made a nervous washing motion with his hands. "Someone on staff does rounds, that is, checks each patient every 15 minutes. She couldn't find Laurel at the last check, so everyone began looking. Laurel is nowhere to be found. It's possible she has been gone for half an hour if she left after the last check."

"Whoa," Jimmy said. "She must've been planning this because she called me to pick her up. Said she was going home today. I thought it was sanctioned."

"When?" Mo asked.

"About forty-five minutes ago."

"What do we do now?" Mo directed her question to the social worker. "I'll cancel the rest of my day."

"We report it to the authorities." Joe told Mo and Jimmy. "And the family, but you already know. Most patients just go home. She might contact you. Why don't you come to my office and give me information about anyplace else she might turn up? He glanced at me then, looking uncertain what to do about the meeting we had scheduled.

"Why don't I wait for you on the unit?" I said, giving up any hope that I would make it to work on time.

Joe agreed and asked Laurel's parents to wait for him. He swiped his name badge over the electronic pad. The lock clicked and once again I passed through the cramped ante room lined with wheelchairs, linen bins, and a cart of picked over lunch trays. At the second door, he let me onto the unit before returning to the parents. As the nurse said to me yesterday, escaping wouldn't be easy, but there was always a way.

Inside, I made my way past the blaring television, and the patients arguing about who changed the channel. The nursing station was a fishbowl surrounded with windows that allowed staff to watch the day area and patients to watch the staff. Right now, the door was closed and most of the workers were huddled, conferring I was sure, about Laurel's disappearance. I knocked for entrance and explained that I had written the detainment papers for Laurel, so the charge nurse could check our office off her list of calls to report the elopement.

A hospital assistant holding a clipboard with patient names described looking for Laurel. A nurse with paisley tattooed arms tried to shush everyone, and another nurse with curly red hair looked franticly around the small room until she found her striped sweatshirt draped over a chair by the door. She put it on and pulled the sleeves until they covered all but the tips of her fingers. Then she reflexively reached for the collar. "Shit," she said. It was just the beginning of an impressive string of expletives.

Everyone stopped talking and looked at her.

"I left my badge clipped to my hoodie. It's gone." She made a valiant display of checking her pockets. All eyes were on her.

"I remember now," the tattooed woman said. "Laurel came into the office. She said she was looking for art supplies.

Just outside the office door, the carpet changed from wavy gray stripes to a plain blue rectangle meant to remind patients not to enter the inner sanctum.

"She must have gotten my badge then."

Everyone was talking again while they determined that Laurel had been wearing gray jeans and a white, long sleeved shirt and might have passed for a hospital employee or a visitor if she chose the moment when the staff who knew her had their attention focused elsewhere. Laurel was smart, and she must have been thinking clearly enough to plan it all out.

I had learned as much as I could on the unit and got a staff person in the dayroom to let me out the locked doors. I looked in the social worker's door. Laurel's parents had left so Joe and I commiserated about how terribly this case was going.

"Do you think Laurel could have killed her therapist?" I asked.

Joe shrugged. "I remember a guy who had killed his roommate, but long after the fact. He didn't seem like a killer by the time I saw him."

"I know," I said. Then I hurried off to the office where Annie and I would now have to meet with Vera and get a bench warrant so the Seattle Police would pick up Laurel if they found her. I hoped they'd be looking as hard as possible. On the sky bridge, I saw Jimmy James lounging in one of the chairs with his legs stretched out and crossed at the ankles, studying his phone. He glanced up and clicked off the screen.

"Mo's gone to check with Laurel's friends," Jimmy said. He didn't have the worried look I'd seen on Mo. He hadn't been through Laurel's first episode of psychosis. According to the paperwork, that time, she'd been found walking down the centerline of Interstate 5 in the middle of the night, paranoid because she thought her friends would kill her. Nor had he been awake night after night the past week trying to keep Laurel safe. "Like her or not, Mo endures."

"What do you mean?"

Jimmy used his fingers to groom his beard while he drew up the memory. "I've known her since she was fifteen years old. Seen her through Laurel's age. She doesn't want to remember those times."

"Did she have mental health problems?" I asked, remembering that she had reported none when I interviewed her.

"Not that. What I mean is Mo was," He searched for a word, "Feral. She was a wild child, but you wouldn't know it to see her now. I bet that red jacket cost $500." He had a misty smile at the memory of the wild Mo. "She doesn't even want to acknowledge those days, so when Laurel has trouble, Mo goes to work. All she does is work and she's taking Laurel on as a project."

I nodded. "When adult kids are ill, it's the parents' job to step back in for a while. Then back off again when they get better. It's a difficult dance to master."

He shrugged. "What she doesn't see is that it's my time to step up and be a father. That's my plan when we find her."

I'd seen parents respond in a lot of different ways when their children were ill—everything from anger at me and the system, to thankfulness. I couldn't read Jimmy James. "I am worried about Laurel too," I said.

Jimmy seemed to sense my thoughts and pulled himself up straight. "You probably think I'm a flake, but don't underestimate me. I've sponsored some real difficult cases in NA, you know, Narcotics Anonymous. They turned their lives around, just like Mo. I don't have to cancel a busy schedule to be there for Laurel. Hey. What's on my schedule is this—I'm going to be at Columbia City Theater tonight and tomorrow. I play the sax and I'm jamming with a band called the Graceful Ox." He eyed my name badge. "Like you, Grace. Laurel was planning to be there. Maybe she will. You could come too."

I reminded him that if Laurel did show up, it was Jimmy's responsibility to get her back to the hospital and said good-bye.

Chapter 6

After Nate was shot, Annie and I were no longer partners. We would meet for lunch once a month and chat at the beginning of the shift when cases were divided up. It hadn't been the same. Today, even with her cold, she made it to work. We waded through the court paperwork for Laurel, then she was back in the field with me. I was secretly elated. Annie was my favorite partner. There was no one I would rather spend time with in a car.

We had an assessment in Skykomish, a tiny river town on the northeast edge of King County. To get there we had to drive out of county then drop south again on Route 2. I drove and Annie, sitting in the passenger seat with a box of Kleenex on her lap, read the case information so we could plan our approach. I sneaked looks at her, trying to tell how she was doing. Her eyes were bloodshot and her face puffy, but she'd washed her hair and looked like anyone with a cold who came to work instead of calling in sick.

"We're seeing a thirty-eight-year-old Caucasian woman with a history of Bipolar Disorder. There's a hospitalization every few years when she's under stress. Otherwise very successful. Works at Amazon." Annie paraphrased the intake. "I guess I'll take the lead."

I found the address on a forested road by the river. The sound of rushing water and smell of pine set the scene. The house was the city couple's weekend cabin on the river—a cabin in the sense that it was log built, a palace in the sense that it looked like 3,000 square feet of professionally designed luxury. The husband opened the door with relief. His wife had trashed the place. Annie and I stepped past the upended tables and broken lamps littering the rugs by the stone fireplace. The woman, in her late thirties was thin with messy short hair wearing sweats and a sequin tank top in a half disheveled, half dressed-for-the-opera look. She had swept the bookcases clean and knelt on the floor searching the debris in the throes of a manic episode. Mental illness didn't spare people based on money or class.

Today the stress was the loss of her job at Amazon. She had probably been having symptoms for a while. The woman pawed through the mess with one hand and waved at her husband with the other. "It's his fault! I told him I didn't want two houses. How can I manage two houses and a job like mine? I don't even have time to eat dinner." The extra energy people loved when a manic episode first began often flipped into anger and irritability.

Annie did the talking. "How long since you've eaten?" Annie had a way with people that made them feel like she really heard them. Next, she asked about sleep.

"I'm up all night every night. I'm working on a project that will revolutionize the industry," she said though Amazon had already revolutionized the sale of everything. "Bezos wants new arms of the business. Healthcare! High-end grocery! Everything people need will be at Amazon because I'm making it."

Her speech was so rapid and pressured that it would be hard to get a word in, but Annie gently steered the conversation. The woman deescalated just by having someone with Annie's calm demeanor talk to her. No wonder she was stressed. Her project had brought anti-trust threats against the company. While Annie talked, I scanned the room. Yes, the woman had lost control but not totally. Across the room, what looked like a million dollars' worth of Chihuly glass sat untouched on glass shelves with diffused lighting. She had only broken things that were replaceable. Always the optimist, I hoped it meant she would decide to cooperate with treatment.

I watched Annie at work, and she looked good. On my first day back in the field after Nate's shooting, my posture was rigid and upright the whole time. I scanned every corner looking for movement or something out of place, any danger I might have missed. The reaction was understandable but didn't help my job. Fortunately, it passed. This evening was perfect for Annie's reentry to work in the field—and successful. The woman from Amazon agreed to let her husband drive her to Evergreen Hospital for a voluntary admission. Maybe Annie was making a comeback.

On the drive back into the city, I asked Annie how she felt. She admitted to a flutter of panic but seemed giddy about how well it had gone. Normally, we would chat about favorite restaurants and books we'd been reading, but now she asked about Laurel's escape from the psych unit. I told her about the nurse with the hoodie and all the details that didn't go into the paperwork. Traffic was thin heading back to the city, but a steady stream of headlights came at us. I felt the pressure building in Annie before I finished the story.

"This is very bad," Annie said. "She's vulnerable."

I just nodded.

"She's still at risk for hurting herself. She's not well enough to be safe in the community." Annie blew her nose into a Kleenex, then shredded it. She spent most of the trip reviewing Laurel's case while I drove, knowing I could never reassure her adequately. Finally, just before she fired up the laptop to get down to work, she added. "Until Marion Warfield's killer is found," her voice caught in her throat. "I have to admit that it could be Laurel."

The lights from the northbound traffic flashed on her face as each car passed. Her fine hair caught the light and set the side of her face in ghostly relief, then darkness. Annie might have been reading about our next evaluation, but my better guess was that she was picturing the sidewalk in front of the old apartment building again. I was right.

"If Laurel doesn't turn up," she said, "I'll go talk to the woman at the Curiosity Shop. I think she'll let me into her apartment."

My own thoughts were about the Cole's court case, but I wasn't ready to mention that. One crisis at a time.

The next night was worse. Annie used to do most of the driving because of my long commute, but now she wanted me to do it again, so I belted into the white Ford and backed out of the parking space.

It was Friday and we were on our way to evaluate a man, Terrance Love, on Yesler Way in the Central District. Yesler stretched three miles between the Puget Sound and Lake Washington. The term Skid Row was coined near our office, in Pioneer Square, back when loggers skidded the first-growth trees down Yesler to where the sawmills were. We left downtown before 5:00 and followed Yesler up and over the hill to the east. I decided to drop down to Lake Washington and the Leschi Market to buy take-out before the evaluation. The best prime rib in the city, according to Annie. She seemed so angelic, it was hard to imagine her gorging on meat and licking her fingers. But this had been our Friday ritual for years. Prime rib dinners during our dinner break, sometimes in a park, weather permitting. Other times in the car, trying not to make too big a mess in the county sedan.

As I pulled out of the angled parking places onto Lake Washington Blvd, the meaty smell from the takeout bag convinced me to eat early. I moved the car to the marina across the street where we could watch the darkening lake and listen to the music of the sailboat riggings in the breeze. Then we'd do our assessment.

"I missed you," I told Annie.

She looked at me seriously. In my stomach, I felt the tension that must be in hers. "This kind of work isn't for me anymore. You know that, Grace."

I nodded and sat quietly, waiting for her to say more.

"I miss you too," she finally said.

"When you get a job as a chaplain, we'll have to find another way to spend time, but it won't be like figuring out a case together." Long silence followed as I chewed the tender meat.

Across from the marina, crows were gathering in the trees by the lake. Hundreds of them preparing to fly south to their evening roosting place in the lowlands near Tukwila. I cleaned my hands with the packaged wipes and started the car and noticed that Annie hadn't eaten much at all. She told me she'd save it for later.

Our evaluation was located in the Central District where the once-strong African American community was now being driven south of the city by rising prices and the onslaught of development started by Microsoft's other founder, Paul Allen. The intake said a man in a boarding house run by a local church had been yelling and kicking the walls. The other residents felt threatened, and the police said there was nothing they could do. The minister who called us was a balding black man wearing a tan leather suitcoat. He paced outside the once-proud home with a broad front porch flanked by Doric columns. I'd heard he was used to dealing with rough cases. The building housed people who were just getting off the streets after long bouts of homelessness. Peeling white paint and a cracked front window made me dream of seeing the building refurbished, but gentrification would drive out the services too. I wondered how long this old place would last.

Inside and upstairs, a pasty-looking man with watery blue eyes and balled fists walked back and forth in a narrow hallway. The worn wooden floor squeaked each time he turned. It was one of those conversions where the house had been broken up into tiny studio apartments with thin wooden doors lining each side of the passage.

"They can't be trusted. Arabs and Mexican Illegals. They steal from me." He turned again. "They've stolen my art! It is worth millions!"

I took the lead today and after introducing myself and my role, I asked him about his art. He paced in front of his door and Annie hung back. I rely on an internal antenna to guide my assessments, what a person needed to hear, their level of anger or fear that could lead to danger. Today, I felt like a Geiger counter with the arrow jumping from side to side wildly. In front, the man I was evaluating and his paranoia, behind; Annie's growing arousal. I felt a panic building in her and wondered who to take care of first. I stepped back to look at the big picture and what I saw was a crowded hallway, and a troubled middle-aged white man. When I imagined it through Annie's eyes it looked a lot like the assessment we did in Ballard that day.

I knew the man had been pacing like this all day. Annie became my priority. Her pupils were dilated and her skin paled. A pulse jumped near her eye and her breathing was fast and shallow.

"Annie, look at me." I gently touched her arm and did the slow breath trick to ground myself. She imitated me and exhaled one slow breath. I've heard advice that when people are faced with bears, they should make themselves big to stay safe. I looked from Terrance Love's eyes to Annie's and made myself very big. They would both rely on me to keep them safe. "Mr. Love," I said, "my partner and I are going to step outside for a minute. I'll be back to talk more."

Then I lightly touched Annie's elbow and guided her out the door and down the rickety steps to the street. I unlocked the door to the county car with a click of the key fob and Annie opened it stiffly and sat in the passenger seat.

"Breathe," I softly ordered. Then with a little less confidence in my voice, I said, "Pray." That was when I saw her head lower and her chest expand. She raised a trembling hand and crossed herself. The muscles in her shoulders let go just a little. "Are you OK to wait here?" She nodded. Her lips were moving in a silent recitation and though I didn't believe much in God myself, I added my own thanks that it was helping Annie. Then, even though it was against all safety protocols, I went back inside and did the evaluation by myself. Mr. Love's actions weren't enough to commit him, but I managed to talk him into taking his evening medications. When I left, he was sitting in his room and beginning to look better.

Chapter 7

All the recent night shifts had thrown off my schedule, making me more alert the later it got. Annie and I said a shy good-bye at the office, not sure what to say about what happened on Yesler. I told her I'd call in the morning. Even though I was running on nerves, I remembered what Jimmy James had said about Laurel turning up at his gig. He struck me as the kind of person who liked to be a caretaker but wasn't up to setting boundaries. I wondered if that was why he suggested I come.

I headed south on Rainier Avenue to the theater. Rainier had a commanding view of the mountain to the south, but after dark it was best avoided. These were my stomping grounds when I was a kid. My neighborhood, Hillman City, was just a few blocks further. It had been middle class until the seventies, then an area of urban blight, then home to Black owned businesses like the Royal Esquire Club. We always knew Columbia City would become popular. Its business district was lined with trees and historic brick-fronted shops. Change came slowly at first but skyrocketing real estate prices were pushing out the older businesses. Drive-by shootings got more media attention now that PCC Natural Market and Molly Moon's Ice Cream had moved in. A lot of the locals had mixed feelings about the gentrification.

The Columbia City Theater was originally a movie house in the 20s. Since then, it had been home to Seattle's burgeoning punk scene and more recently hosted everyone from Macklemore and Lewis to a weekly burlesque show done in drag. The music venue was fronted by the Bourbon Bar. I found parking in front, a sure sign that the music was over for the night. A poster for a band called Graceful Ox flanked the door, but Laurel's father wasn't included in the photo. I decided to check the bar and, after a long workday, put on lip gloss and let my hair out of the restricting pins that held it up.

The bar was old with ornate dark wood, but the smell was more stale beer than bourbon. I recognized Jimmy James' slicked back hair and tats even though his back was turned. He moved like he spent a lot of time working out and his musculature impeded his flexibility. He was talking to a hipster in a trilby and horn rim glasses.

"It's Grace, but not the Ox," he said when he noticed me. He was nursing a tumbler of Pepsi and tapping an unlit cigarette on the bar.

"Hi." The barstool on his other side was empty so I took a seat. Coming to a bar at midnight in search of a missing psychiatric patient was ludicrous. "My mother's house is just down the street from here, so I decided to stop by on my way." My statement was part truth, part fiction. I wasn't on my way to my mom's cold, empty house.

The bartender was a bony, redheaded woman in a leather skirt. I tried to order wine, but she steered me to an Old Log Cabin Bourbon because it was local. She insisted that wine would make me too tired at this hour. I figured it did make sense to drink whiskey at a place called the Bourbon Bar.

"Are you looking for Laurel?" Jimmy asked.

"You said she might come."

"She hasn't been by, but I just talked to Mo. She's…"

A second man with disconcerting mutton chop sideburns and a guitar case came in and put his hand on Jimmy's shoulder and leaned in close. "This your newest groupie, Jimmy?" I could smell old liquor rising from his pores and it didn't make me crave a drink of my own.

"Hey man, cool it," Jimmy said. "The lady is a mental health evaluator. She's trying to help find my daughter. Laurel ran away from Harbor-Zoo today."

"Oh man, that's good she doesn't look like your type."

"None of this is good…"

The guy kept going without listening. "The one you met when you were playing at El Corazon was a real project. Maybe she should have been at the Zoo." The guy slurred his words, too drunk to show empathy for Jimmy's daughter. The bartender put down my drink and before I had a chance to pick it up, the guy with the sideburns grabbed it and tossed it back in one gulp. The woman scolded him and said she'd pour me a fresh one. Jimmy grabbed his Pepsi and his cigarette and waved me toward the door. "Hold it back for a minute. Miss Grace and I are going outside to talk."

"He likes to take in real whack jobs. He's good at it," the drunk guy said as we were leaving. "Told me his ex-wife was a street kid when he met her. Now she owns a million-dollar restaurant."

Outside on the sidewalk, Jimmy struck a match and lit his cigarette. The smell of sulfur and fresh tobacco hit the cold air and smoke curled up to the bar's lighted sign. He squinted into the smoke. "Don't listen to him. I don't like drunks, but he's a good guitar player. He used to work for Mo and found the story how I met her titillating."

"She owns a restaurant?" I asked, remembering her white coat that evening I first met her.

"The Elevated Beast," he said. "A nose to tail place. Heavy on the meat."

It reminded me of the prime rib I'd shared with Annie. "I heard of that," I said. "It just opened out in Duvall."

"That's her second location. Anyway. I'm sure Mo wasn't easy to work for, so the guy likes to think of Mo as kind of crazy herself."

"A project?" I asked and noticed that his manner of speaking changed when he was talking to me.

"Hey, a lot of people had a hard life as kids. I was like that and now that I'm in the program," he said referring to one of the Twelve-Step Programs. "I'm a sponsor. We all help each other out. It's my mission. Anyway, I talked to Mo. She called all of Laurel's friends and told them to be on the lookout for her. She went by Laurel's apartment too. No answer there and neither of us has a key. The girl who manages the apartments checked—no Laurel. But she wouldn't let Mo in." Jimmy looked stressed now. "What happens when they find her?"

I told him about the court order to return his daughter to the hospital. I didn't mention Laurel's confession and the complications that brought—a bar was no place for that conversation. Instead, I reassured him that Laurel would turn up soon.

He gave me a serious smile and said he figured I was right. We went inside, and the bartender handed me a fresh drink. I sipped the amber liquid. The bartender pointed out the bourbon's caramel notes while the men talked music until my limbs felt unmanageable. I'd never make the hour-long drive home in this condition. I really was going to sleep in my mother's empty house. I called Frank to tell him I'd spend the night in the city and received a decidedly cool response. Another thing to deal with in the morning.

The Rainier Valley and its local schools had been rough when I was growing up. Mom worked as a clerk in the pharmacy on Wilson Avenue—it couldn't have paid well. I always wondered where she got the money to buy a house. Still, it was the era of the Boeing Bust when the airplane manufacturer laid off its workforce and a billboard popped up saying, "Will the last person leaving Seattle turn out the lights." Real estate prices hadn't always been the fastest rising in the nation.

Mom's little brown bungalow was set back from the street and blocked from view by a false cypress and two cedars someone had planted as tiny shrubs back in the thirties. Now they topped forty feet giving it a little-cabin-in-the-woods feel that carried inside to the worn fir floors and over-filled rooms. I realized now that it was a smaller city version of my grandparents' house in Duvall where Frank and Nell and I lived now. The lights in the front windows were on a timer and although it was bright, the air was musty inside. The smell of burned dust filled the air when I turned on the furnace.

The week before, I'd brought a load of boxes and left them in the middle of the living room floor. Now, I walked around the cardboard to assess the job of sorting and packing before we put the house up for sale. None of her belongings called me to take them home. My grandparents' house was filled with the family history: Victorian rockers and embroidered samplers. Mom had filled her house with faux Americana. I liked her window full of colored glass vases that played with the light, but I didn't want them. Too much dusting. I'd probably call a company to hold an estate sale. Still, there were family albums to locate.

I climbed the steep steps to the room under the eaves. At the top of the steps, I turned on the light and was startled by a cloud of tiny buff-colored moths that fluttered and disappeared so quickly I might have imagined them. My avoidance had gone on too long. I resolved to focus on wrapping up the house.

One last moth circled the room and vanished. I'd never seen the kind that eats woolens but suspected that's what I had. The thought of packing up grew more intimidating. I checked drawers, then looked in the closet with out of season clothes and beat the hangered jackets with my hand. That displaced a moth or two, but I didn't think I'd found the source. I hit the stained easy chairs where we'd watched TV with dinner on our laps and circled around to an old steamer trunk tucked in a corner. I opened the lid and stepped back in revulsion.

Something, once woven, now unrecognizable, had turned to dust. I didn't know a thing about the life cycle of moths, but the thought of white larvae gave me the creeps even though they had hatched and flown away. I bumped the trunk down the steps and dragged it out to the covered front porch where I slammed and locked the door on the pests. I washed my hands longer than necessary and finally crawled into the narrow bed in the room that had been mine growing up. I wished I'd gotten a glass of wine back at the Bourbon Bar.

In the morning, I wanted to sleep in and tried to ignore my phone, first pinging, then ringing at my bedside. I had a text and two calls. The text was from Nell: reminding me that we were volunteering for the annual Point in Time Count when cities and towns all over King County tried to record the number of homeless people sleeping outside between midnight and 4:00 a.m. on a cold night. In the foothills, our first frost was due any day, especially with the clear weather. I was glad Nell and I had the common concern. I also figured my sleep schedule could take anything now. Another wakeful night. No problem.

I called Frank who wasn't too happy that I'd be missing yet another night at home in bed.

Then Annie. Her voice was hard to read, and I decided to wait for her bring up yesterday's panic.

"Is there any news on Laurel James?" she asked.

I filled her in on my fruitless talk with Jimmy James.

"I'll go to her place above the Curiosity Shop then," she said.

I worried about it setting off her alarms. "Do you want company? I slept at my mom's house."

"You did?" She paused but didn't ask why. We were skirting a lot of issues. "No, I'm good." A long silence grew on the phone. Annie finally broke it. "I'm sorry about yesterday. I wasn't there for you."

"You knew you weren't ready for the field."

"God damn it," she said. "Oh hell. I'll never be ready for the field again." Those were strong words for Annie. She didn't swear and often told me that the expletives used by younger men on our team disturbed her to the point of tears. She was as old fashioned as my grandmother in not using the Lord's name in vain.

"Are you sure you can't get an extension on your light duty?"

"Forget it. I'm scheduled to do evaluations in the hospital this evening. But really, I just don't know."

"You'll figure it out," I said, hoping to calm her.

"I don't know," she repeated, impatient. "I've got to go Grace."

That was it for our phone call.

My usual morning routine was to linger over breakfast and read the New York Times online, but I hated reading on my phone and there was no coffee at my mother's house. A cup of stale English Breakfast tea would have to do. I leaned back in the chair and gazed out the picture window at the back garden, struggling with my thoughts. I tried to tell myself I had forgiven Mom for neglecting me when she was depressed but had to admit I was still critical, all the time.

I figured it was time to face the steamer trunk on the front porch. Armed with a pair of rubber gloves and a Hefty garbage bag from under the kitchen sink, I lifted the lid and sorted. Out came the tattered woolen which I barely recognized as a weaving Frank and I brought back from Peru. The ghost of warp and weft showed the rust-colored background, lined with orange and rose shapes chosen for Mom, but she had a penchant for putting pretty things away for a later date. Not a good idea in this case. I shoved everything made of fabric into the garbage bag.

Finally, I pulled out an unstrung porcelain doll and three department store boxes that I recognized. They were filled with Saran-wrapped pocket diaries my mother had kept since she was a girl. All but one carefully stored. She'd tried to burn it before she died. I took the diaries back to the kitchen and reheated my tea in the microwave. The diary I picked was full of high school friends and clothes and dating. She'd met my father then. It must have been a good year for her. I tossed it back into the box, frustrated that I'd missed it.

I told myself to think of a good memory and didn't have to look far. Mom's garden was beautiful, her pride. I grabbed my coat and went out to the bench swing sheltered by a vine-covered lattice and rocked back and forth, comforted by the creak of the rusty chains. Frank and I had cared for the garden when Mom slowed down and ever since. Dusting her vases might be beyond me, but I wouldn't dream of neglecting her plants.

When I was a girl, the yard was full of flowers backed by the small pine: Shasta daisies and old-fashioned purple iris. My favorite was a peaches-and-cream striped rose. The rose was still there, but as the pine grew taller, it shaded the garden and the hungry roots spread out and stole the nourishment the rose needed. Now the rose was leggy and sparse. I pictured taking it home and giving it sun and lots of scrapings from the chicken house.

More memories followed. By the time Nell was growing up, Mom's depression had lifted. She took up sewing and lunched with friends. She turned into the sweet grandmother who baked peanut butter cookies decorated with fork-tine cross hatches.

I remembered the day we hosted the funeral dinner for my grandfather in the house he'd built. It was Mom who encouraged us to move to Duvall. I had spent summers there as a child and got most of my nurturing from my grandparents. I used to think that Mom was relieved when I was gone, but that day, she told me how safe she had felt there and seemed at a loss for words, she shook her head trying to say more but nothing came. She only told the stories of running barefoot on the path to Cherry Creek behind the house, making doll houses out of bark and sword ferns. The same games I had played. That was the feeling we wanted to pass on to Nell. We agreed on that.

When I finished my tea, I gathered my things and put the diaries in a paper bag I found under the sink. I had little desire to read more but maybe Nell would.

Chapter 8

The All-Home Count was a hopeful sounding name. But, of course, far too many people were not home and given prices in our county, they weren't getting a home any time soon. The count took on special meaning for me because so many of King County's homeless suffered from mental illness.

Duvall's Main street, usually empty at midnight, filled with volunteers coming to help. I now recognized The Elevated Beast as Mo James' recently opened restaurant in the upstairs of an old wood frame building. Dim lights glowed in the mullioned windows, and though it was closed, I imagined intimate diners at tables with flickering candles.

Nell had been with friends all day and spent the evening in her cabin. I was glad to have this time with her, but she seemed quiet and withdrawn. Her shiny chartreuse coat made it hard to disappear, but she seemed to be trying, with her hands shoved in the pockets and a black watch cap pulled low over her eyes.

We let ourselves into the old library, a little red house, now the Duvall Visitors Center. I thought I could still smell the books here even though they had moved to the modern building across the road. I waved at neighbors settling in at round tables set with maps and plates of homemade cookies. An aluminum coffee maker steamed in the corner. We grabbed some coffee and joined Danny, a carpenter friend of Frank's who lived on Stossel Creek Road. He had a long, braided beard that I always worried would get caught in the power tools—definitely, one of the counterculture guys of the valley.

"Here's our territory," he said pointing to the photocopied map on our table. We would be working the area west from Main Street to the Snoqualmie River and included McCormick Park and its riverside trails.

After Annie's panic attack the night before, potential triggers worried me. Nell and I had joined the All-Home Count after the deaths of our neighbor and another man at the river—our small effort to help. It hadn't affected Nell before, but she seemed off tonight. I leaned over and said quietly, "Are you okay about counting there? It's where Martin and Alfred Mallecke were killed."

She gave me a dismissive look. "Are you okay with it?"

"It's fine," I said. I'd been there a dozen times since. Neither of us were wired like Annie, it was just that Nell wasn't her usual self.

Carl Ring, the police chief, wandered over to say hello. The buttons of his uniform shirt strained with what seemed like an extra ten pounds he'd gained.

"Hey, you two," he said, leaning over to grab a macaroon. "I'm hoping we can get started early. The news is predicting some big windstorm by five AM. Don't know how they can be so precise but if it comes early, we're in a world of trouble. Can you help, Nell?" He held out a clipboard with the names of all the volunteers. "If you let me know when most of the people are here, we can get started."

Nell left her coat on the chair, but still wore the dark cap. She checked off the names. Carl seemed to think we had enough and called us to order. "You'll be working in groups for safety and each table has a leader."

A redheaded volunteer fireman joined our table and pointed to his nametag. Our leader. I was eager to get moving, but Carl gave the same instructions every year. We were instructed not to bother people, to respect them as if they were in their homes, because they were—even if it was a tent, a tarp, or a car.

Danny and the firefighter got involved in a fly-fishing discussion and lagged, but I figured they counted for safety because they were in hollering distance. The weather was clear and cold with no storm in sight. We started in McCormick Park and walked down to the river where the dark water moved almost silently along the sandy beach. Nell found a couple suitcases under a sheet of muddy plastic hidden down a path in the underbrush, but no people. We didn't venture too far from Danny and the firefighter. I paused on the riverbank and surprised a deer.

"How did your talk with your supervisor go yesterday? Will you come back to the same job?" I asked as Nell and I walked, our feet crunching on the packed dirt trail that split the river from the valley fields.

She studied the beams from our flashlights sweeping ahead, then slowed. "I'm not sure that is going to work out."

"But you love your job. I thought he was being supportive."

"I don't think so." She said in a tight voice that meant she did not want to talk about it right now. Our teammates were coming closer, maybe she was afraid they'd overhear. We passed the place where Alfred Mallecke had been found, and Nell turned up to the road that ran behind the Main Street shops. Tent cities were common in Seattle, but in the county, people without homes were more likely to be sleeping in cars or too far in the woods to find.

Nell studied some parked cars as we walked. She inclined her head toward an old silver Honda but stayed a respectful distance away. "I think someone is sleeping in there."

The trick was to look for the steamy windshield and condensation. Even in the darkness we could tell that boxes and loose clothing filled this car to its ceiling, as if the owner wanted to hold on to a previous life. Next, we found a Toyota with cardboard covering the windows like a semblance of curtains. I longed for the days of my youth when steamy windows meant teens exploring the joy of sex.

I kept my voice quiet as we walked. "He said no?" I tried one more time.

"Let's not talk about this." She shoved her hands deep into the pockets of her parka.

We checked more parked cars. So far, our count was two, which seemed high for a small area so close to town. We wound to the end of our territory then doubled back along the same street. From about a block away, I could see a man dressed in a hooded sweatshirt under a heavy coat. He leaned against an old green SUV and the tip of a cigarette glowed bright when he drew on it. He studied the backs of the shops. I looked for Danny and the firefighter who were supposed to be with us, but they were lagging. Nell and I kept to the far side of the street, but we must not have been discrete enough.

"What are you looking at?" He demanded.

I kept my distance and pointed to the sticky nametag I'd been given. "We are with the All-Home Count," and gave him a lot of distance and explained the process. He looked Latino, maybe 50, with gray flecked hair under his hood and black-framed glasses. His face was angular and handsome.

"I'm not homeless, I'm traveling and needed rest." He protested in a growl, then glanced at the businesses behind my shoulder one last time.

"Sorry to bother you, sir," Nell said, and we continued past him, but we had already done the bothering and he ground out his cigarette, jumped in the car and spun gravel away. The smell of burned rubber from his tires stung my nose. XLM 297. I don't know why, but I made a point of remembering the number on his muddy license plate.

I turned to see what he had been watching. It was the one light along the back windows of Main Street. A lone figure moved about. From shape alone, I could tell that it was Laurel's mother, Mo, in the restaurant. It was after two a.m. The place had probably been closed for hours. Maybe it was prep for the next day.

Warmly lit windows at night always drew me in. I imagined parents and children together in the evening, dining, watching TV on the couch—as if the scene was a snapshot of a happy family. I wanted to be like them. Nell and I worked our way closer to Main Street and the window the man had been watching. As we got closer, I realized why Mo James had seemed familiar when I met her at the hospital. I'd seen her in a Seattle Magazine in a picture with both Mo and her daughter before I met them—the renowned chef from the city opening her second bistro in Duvall. I could see the top third of the kitchen, a clutter of stainless-steel pots and utensils hung from the ceiling. Mo was in a white jacket like the one I'd seen her in before. She moved with more energy than I could imagine at the hour, moving a heavy pot, probably to the cooler, then flicked off the lights. An image of a good mother—she'd put her troubled past behind her—but not at this moment a happy family. I pulled my eyes away.

The men on our team finally walked protectively up behind us. "Was somebody bothering you?" the firefighter asked.

"No, I think we bothered him," I answered, and they went back to their conversation, laughing a little too loudly to be respectful of anyone sleeping nearby.

The questions surrounding Laurel, her family and her therapist followed me even here. I turned to Nell. "Do you think that man was watching the restaurant?"

She nodded but seemed too preoccupied to care. Even under her parka, I could tell that Nell's shoulders were hiked up with tension. We finished out territory just before 4:00 am and walked up to the community center. Inside, a long table had been set up with steam pans full of sausage and milky gravy. Pyramids of homemade biscuits filled platters. This menu was an annual tradition for the Count. My mouth watered when I smelled the perfect comfort food after being up all night.

Nell stopped in the doorway and took my arm. "I quit my job."

Chapter 9

Nell and I stepped away from the community center door where other volunteers filtered in. When we had plenty of space, I asked. "Why are you quitting?"

"My supervisor. My ex-supervisor," she corrected herself, "Came on to me."

Now her responses made sense. "Oh Nell, damn. What happened?"

"You know how men do." She took my arm as if to steady herself and talked with her eyes closed. "It started with the bump of the knee, the brush of the hand. Then he came right out and said that if we got together, he'd hold my job for me. I'm not naïve. I know how the world works. It sickens me, Mom. I don't know why it makes me so sick." She opened her eyes and her voice gained volume. The anger was coming now.

I pulled her into a hug, and she bumped her head against my shoulder again and again. I think she wanted to do it much harder. I let her talk now that the dam had broken. The air was cold and brown leaves rattled on the street trees as the first winds blew up the street. Maybe a storm really was coming.

"I do know why I hate it so much," she said. "Because now I think that's why I've had this job all along. What little Anglo girl gets a job as a Spanish interpreter. I look back and I think this is what he had in mind ever since he hired me."

I felt a chill. Social media was still rife with women telling their stories, long after the #metoo movement about women who had been harassed on the job hit the news. Bad behavior didn't change that fast, though.

63

"Good for you for leaving," I said. "Are you going to report him?"

Her eyes teared up, "I haven't decided yet." She described the usual dilemma. Would reporting him haunt her if she still worked in the field?

I wished I could do something. I couldn't. The rising winds swept the sidewalk and peppered our faces with grit. The weather forecast had been right, and the storm was right on time. I ducked inside to turn in our numbers, then Nell and I skipped the biscuits and gravy and headed home. By the time we reached Cherry Valley Road, tree branches were flailing, and the first fat drops of rain hit the windshield.

We ran inside. Now that Nell had told me what was wrong, she was on a talking jag and circled every interaction they'd had. I made toast and put a cup of chamomile tea in front of her. Wind and rain whipped the windows with a force as furied as her thoughts. We sat, elbows on the kitchen table as she jumped from one memory to the next, looking for intentions she might have picked up earlier.

"Try not to blame yourself," I soothed, even though I knew it was part of the process she would be going through. I'd been worried about the wrong triggers tonight. By 6:00 AM my chin, propped on my hand, slipped when I nodded off. I woke with a start. "I'm sorry."

"It's okay." Nell got up and carried our dishes to the sink, then sensing my concern, stopped to rub my back. "Really. I'll write in my journal."

I crawled off to bed. Nell had moved to the couch and scribbled furiously. The winds still rattled the windows.

Sleep came right away but didn't last. My battery-operated clock said it was 9:00. When I reached to turn on the lamp, nothing happened. The wind had stopped, but it had taken the power with it. I padded downstairs where Frank motioned at the useless coffee maker. "Let's drive into town for breakfast."

The valley, with fewer big trees to take down power lines, might have electricity, but I was worried about Nell and started to give Frank the short version of what she'd said.

"I know," he said. "She was still awake when I got up, but I finally got her to settle."

I wasn't satisfied until I checked on her myself and saw Nell asleep with one arm covering her eyes as if she could stop herself from seeing what had happened.

"Okay, I want to try the Elevated Beast," I said. I was still looking for Laurel.

The power outage had skipped town. Everything was open. Beside the gift shop on Main Street, a flight of stairs led to The Elevated Beast. I wondered if Mo would be there after her late night and wondered if I would finally get some sausage and gravy.

A line of diners snaked past the host's desk and down the stairs for the busy Sunday brunch. We waved to a few familiar faces. Duvall had grown as quickly as Seattle, adding new subdivisions for workers from Redmond's tech firms. The Beast's atmosphere was country meets modern. A yoke for oxen dominated one wall like a sculpture. Gray siding contrasted with glossy black tables and chairs. Along the back, windows looked over the valley. I knew the windows continued into the kitchen where I'd seen Mo working the night before.

Frank put our names on the waiting list and brought back menus. "Braised Boar, Eggs Benedict," he said with a skeptical tone that turned appreciative when he got to the House Cured Applewood Bacon. He'd never make it as a vegetarian. "I picked up a dinner menu too. You can get duck hearts, foie gras or pork belly at night." He read a detailed provenance of each.

"Local Venison Sausage," I read from the breakfast menu.

"It's like the Portlandia episode where every piece of meat is introduced by name." He spoke. "This is Bill, your local deer."

"Payback. He ate my roses last year."

We joked and prepared for a long wait when I felt a hand on my arm. Mo James, wearing a fresh white jacket, didn't look any the worse for wear after her own long night. "Grace," she said. "Do you live in the area?"

"We live behind town," I told her and introduced Frank.

Mo scanned the wait list and crossed off our names even though they were still at the bottom. "I bought a house in North Bend a couple years ago, with a view of Mount Si. That's why I opened here in the valley."

"I heard about your restaurant, but it's the first we've come." I decided to let her be the one to bring up Laurel if she wanted to. It didn't take long.

For a moment, she looked expectant. "I'd hoped you were here with some news of Laurel. I'm so worried."

Frank studied his menu to give us freedom to talk.

"I'm sorry," I said. "The police are looking, but parents usually hear before we do. I hope Laurel will contact you herself."

"That's what I was afraid of. I'm the wrong parent." She scanned the room. "Let me find you the next table."

Before I could protest, she ushered us through the busy room, past a display of pumpkin and blue squash, to a table for four by the window. Last night's storm had blown over. October clouds clung to the valley, back lit by a weak sun from the east.

"Wrong parent?" I asked, wanting to hear more.

"I raised Laurel by myself. Jimmy had no income, so there was no child support. Working in the restaurant business makes it difficult to parent because of bad hours and stress. I was yelling at her half the time. Now Jimmy shows up and Laurel pushes me away. He's the shiny new toy. It's natural for her to want to know him, but I hate it. I know it's envy." Mo found a spot of food on her white jacket and tried to rub it out. I noticed her hands and forearms were scarred from knife slips and cooking burns. "Jimmy's heart is in the right place, but I'm afraid he'll sabotage her treatment."

"Really?" I'd wondered about that.

"Jimmy always said that insanity is the only sane reaction to an insane society."

Mo pushed in my chair as I took my seat. "It's a quote," I told her, "Thomas Szasz. He was the psychiatrist who influenced the anti-psychiatry movement in the 60s."

He'd believed that the medical model, especially involuntary treatment, was a form of social control—which could be true, but everyone I knew in the field worked to prevent that.

Mo gave a small laugh. "I should have known Jimmy didn't think it up himself. Idealism is fine—until your daughter is sinking into paranoia."

A waitress motioned Mo for help, but instead of going, Mo sank down in the third chair at the table. "Jimmy has a history of springing girls from treatment," she said.

For a minute, I thought Mo was going to say he had sprung her from treatment, but that wasn't the story.

"When I was fifteen, I was a runaway. A bunch of us lived in an abandoned building on Pike Street. Jimmy was the oldest and he was our mother hen. Long before he got clean and sober, he was into rescuing people. There was a girl in our squat who was sent to the hospital. She bruised her face by banging her head so often. She never slept. But, if you talked to her, she listened like there was no one else in the world. She was so smart. She could have been anything she wanted."

Not unlike Laurel, I thought.

"The hospital found her a group home and she was doing better. Jimmy talked her into coming back to us. Of course, sex probably had something to do with that one. Jimmy thought his love could save her. It was a disaster. She went off medications and never made it back to the group home. She was in the hospital for a year after that." A million emotions played across Mo's face.

For a moment, it looked like she was going to say more, but the waitress came to the table and whispered something frenzied in her ear. Mo placed her hands on the table, ready to push off. "This is a busy time. Anyway, I worry. I wouldn't be surprised if he thought he could help her more than the professionals. She's an adult, but I still try to protect her." Then Mo was gone, striding across the room to take charge.

Her words touched me both professionally and personally. I had a long history of over protecting and since the conversation had turned to daughters, I asked Frank how he'd finally gotten Nell to settle down.

"I gave her the diaries you brought home from your mom's. She'd worn herself out by then. She put down her journals and took Rose's to bed with her. Have you read them?"

The waitress brought our plates before I could answer. I studied the venison sausage and wondered if it would bring me the comfort I'd hoped for last night after the count. "I read about when she was a teenager and met my father, but since I don't remember him, it just made me feel lonely. I stopped." Unlike Laurel, I'd given up on knowing my other parent.

I cut a piece of sausage, added a homemade biscuit, and wiped it through the perfectly browned gravy. I couldn't help wishing that I'd had a mother who cooked like this, even though I knew Laurel's childhood reality sounded as lonely as mine. Frank touched my hand, said the bacon was a hit too.

I watched the clouds break up over the valley. The man with the green SUV hadn't returned, but Mo needed to know he'd been there. When we finished our meals, I stopped to thank Mo. "Last night around 3:00 AM. My daughter and I were down by the river for the homeless count. Your restaurant lights were still on and you were working."

"I was. I got behind schedule when Laurel was ill. I'm still trying to catch up."

"There was a man out there watching your window. When he saw Nell and me, he took off—as if he didn't want to be seen."

She took a slow breath and became incredibly calm.

I described the man with the black glasses and asked if she knew anyone like that.

"I'm not sure," she answered before rushing off to help another customer, "but I think someone has been watching me for a while now."

On our drive home, dark-bellied clouds scudded across the valley leaving behind patches of vibrant blue sky. Last night's rain had collected in the low-lying fields and now reflected the yellows and oranges of leaves on trees. The late October sun arced low in the south, lighting the fenceposts in high relief. The lambs that had taken their first tentative steps in the fields had now grown and probably ended up on Mo James' menu. A cloud now hid the sun, and the fall colors dimmed so quickly I could feel winter coming.

On the curve in the highway near our house, we passed a big Asplundh Tree Removal truck followed by another from Puget Sound Energy giving hope that the electricity would soon be back. At home, the light switches worked, the furnace fan clicked on, and Frank settled at the kitchen table with the *New York Times*. I prowled the house restlessly. My sleep schedule was a mess, and I hadn't cleaned or even looked at the mail. I picked up the pile on the desk and sorted the catalogues from bills I hoped weren't overdue.

My hand stopped at an envelope with the logo belonging to Benjamin and Beard Attorneys. From time to time, I was called upon to testify in detention cases when there were no other witnesses, but I was afraid I knew what this was. Ever since I heard about the lawsuit on the radio, I'd expected this. I tore open the envelope. In the instant I read the Coles' names on the form, I saw the gun, Nate's fall, and my attempt to stanch his bleeding flash red. A deposition was scheduled for the next Friday. I would be giving pretrial evidence under oath. The hospital was certainly hoping the family would settle out of court. If they wanted me, they'd probably call Annie too.

If the letter gave me a flashback, it would be worse for Annie, but when I punched in her number, it went straight to voicemail. I urged her to call me and wondered if she'd been called to testify too.

Then I was too distracted to pay bills and wondered if Nell was awake yet. Fresh coffee and crumbs on the toaster told me she was, so I headed out to see how she was feeling this morning. During her teenage years, Nell had moved into the cedar clad cottage perched on the pond across the garden from our house. The gingkoes, the bamboo, and Japanese maples I once planted had grown into a mature garden. I knocked on the frosted glass door and opened it when Nell called "Come in."

Nell stood in front of the mirror in her orange and black striped pajama bottoms and one of Frank's old shirts. She wielded a pair of silver barber scissors and long strands of her dark hair fell to the floor. My first impulse was to yell, "Stop!" fearing this was an unhealthy response to the harassment.

Nell turned and pointed with the shears. "Don't say it," she whispered as if she could read my mind.

"Right."

On second thought, I decided her haircut wasn't such a bad idea. Nell and I had been trimming Frank's hair for years. We had some skills and Nell often marked life events with a change of style. She'd gone asymmetrical this morning with a chin length bob on one side and a close-to-the-scalp cut on the other. "I'm going to buzz it here," she said touching the short side.

"Want help?" I asked. "I can get that side and the back."

She nodded. "You have long hair, so you may not know. Men bug you less when you have short hair."

"I do know," I said. "I cut mine about ten years ago. Remember?"

"Did it stop the cat calls every time you walked down the street? *Hey baby. Smile...*"

"They did stop," I laughed even though it wasn't funny. "I thought I was just getting older, but they started up as soon as I grew my hair back."

"Fuck them." Nell slapped the scissors on the shelf in front of the mirror and glared at her reflection.

"Not the way they had in mind either," I said and took up the clippers, glad to see her spunkiness coming back. "Which guard should I use?"

"Number two."

"This is going to look great. Maybe you can do some dye too." I ran my fingers through the long part. The clippers hummed when I clicked them on. I swooped over her ear. "Aside from the haircut, how do you feel about yesterday?"

"First, I felt sick, then angry. My brain was just circling, so I decided to leave it."

"Angry is a fine place to be for now."

"I started reading Grandma's diaries," she said.

"Your dad told me."

Nell and I made eye contact in the mirror, then we both looked at the futon and the pocket diaries piled on top of the medieval art books she'd bought to prep for her trip. Those were fanned open to paintings of demons and disease. I recognized one by Hieronymus Bosch showing flames of hell and naked figures in tortured poses. Had Nell been focused on the grotesque before her boss bothered her?

"How are the diaries?" I set down the clippers and rested my hands on Nell's shoulders.

"I can't believe you didn't read them."

Her voice was accusing. I rubbed her head with a towel to free the loose hairs, then brushed her shirt to give myself time to think. Finally, I sank onto the futon next to the dark art. "I started reading one when I found them at Mom's house, but it just made me angry. I understand Mom's depression now, but back then she withdrew, and I was left to raise myself."

"You're still angry," Nell said. "You never told me that her mother died in Northern State Hospital."

My brain froze because I had somehow known this once and forgotten. It felt strange. "The mental institution?"

Nell picked up one of the diaries and passed it to me—the burned leather book with a sheaf of letters and loose pages inside breaking its back. "It's still readable. She ripped pages out too."

I opened the powdery cover and inside, found one moth, perfectly preserved. "She threw this away when she got sick. I pulled it out of the garbage."

"I think she didn't want anyone to read it. That's why I started here." She picked up the stray pages and held them like they were electric. "Then I found a death certificate for Lucy Cooper. Grandma Rose's real mother, Lucy."

"Ah," I said, struggling to imagine my young mother finding and saving that memento. "They told me once that Lucy died of a brain tumor when Mom was in grade school." That was when Mom came to live in Duvall with Lucy's childless sister and her husband who soon adopted her—the couple I knew as my grandparents. I guess that was why Mom felt so safe here. "She did say Northern State. People with brain tumors can have psychotic symptoms, just like the people I see now. I didn't think much about it at the time. Maybe because I was young then—other things were on my mind."

"You never thought to tell me. Mom, really? Kids need to know about their families." Her words reminded me of what Laurel had said about meeting her family. Nell ran her hand back and forth over the newly shorn side of her head. She passed me the blurred photocopy of her death certificate.

"Lucy Cooper died in 1950."

"Northern State," I repeated, like I was in a trance. She was right. I felt like I'd been hypnotized by my grandparents' silence. Or denial. Northern was a big state psychiatric hospital at the edge of the North Cascades. It had closed in the seventies after medications and deinstitutionalization favored community care. "Grandma called it a sanitorium. It made sense." I set the paper down. "What doesn't make sense is that I never thought about it, even when I took up a career in mental health. I didn't ask what happened when Lucy was institutionalized."

Nell's shorn hair still littered the floor. She looked at the papers while I told her what little I remembered about the brain tumor story. Then she passed the death certificate back to me. It looked like it had been folded and handled a million times. "Read."

I reached to turn on the lamp and squinted at the blurry script. The cause of death was a heart attack. No brain tumor was mentioned. Under Secondary Conditions it listed Involutional Melancholia. With Psychosis.

"I looked it up," Nell said. "It's what they used to call a depression that starts in your forties or fifties, so she was probably okay until then. People can get paranoid or think something is wrong with their bodies. Or hear voices."

"She was only 49." I sagged. "I'm sure they thought the brain tumor story was more acceptable."

I thought about the anger I'd carried. The sadness of my family was just starting to sink in. I tried to imagine the woman I'd seen in photographs hearing voices or believing strange things. I'd spent my career working with people like that. It could happen to anyone. Now I tried to imagine my mother seeing it as a child.

"I'm more surprised Grandma Rose never told you," Nell said. "All the years you worked with people with the same problems. It's no more surprising that you conveniently forgot."

"There was so much stigma then. Even more than now. I really can't believe I never asked more questions." I felt deflated, like my body had lost the starch that usually held me up. "Questions were met with an unbearable silence. So unbearable I couldn't even remember."

"Your grandma could be a stone wall," Nell said. "I remember that about her."

"Like it hurt her. She was just so stoic."

Nell gave me a look that told me how much I'd carried on that tradition. She touched the diaries. Years of diaries. "Maybe we can find out more."

I shuddered in my own version of the stone wall. I'd had all I could take of family secrets for the moment. I didn't have the energy. I looked out the big window that framed the pond. Fallen leaves floated at the water's edge and in that moment, a great blue heron, a bird that could have inspired one of the hellish paintings, swooped in and came away with a fish.

Nell tucked the papers into the diary and stacked it with the rest. "I'll do the reading."

"Thanks," I said and swept up the remnants from her haircut before I left. Outside, the air was scrubbed clean from the storm, but the garden was flattened. The wind had brought down the stubbornly clinging leaves, branches, and a few narrow saplings.

I let myself in through the kitchen and the screen door, unneeded this time of year, slapped shut behind me. My grandmother hated the sound and had taught me to close it quietly, a habit I hadn't carried forward when Frank and I took over the house. To my left were pegs for coats and the drying rack that had aired everything from dish towels to laundry in its warm position next to the old wood-fired cook stove we'd have been using if the power had stayed out. I wrapped my arms around myself like a kid. Some memory was close. Standing here listening to my mother and grandmother talking in hushed voices about something I wasn't meant to hear. I couldn't grasp it.

Chapter 10

Annie hadn't returned my call. It wasn't like her.

I texted, *Where are you?* And later, *Are you OK?* She had probably been called to the deposition too. I pictured her sitting in the chair by the bay window sick, not eating or answering her phone. When I still hadn't heard from her in an hour, I drove into Seattle, determined to see her. She still wasn't picking up her phone when I arrived. I resorted to pitching pebbles at the glass like in the old days.

"Annie!" I called from the sidewalk, but her face never appeared. I couldn't help but worry. Seeing her panic at work had shaken loose a memory from when we were students. One night, after sharing a bottle of wine, she talked about the day her aunt died. She described the hollow sound of the car striking her aunt's body in agonizing detail. Annie said that she felt that angels were there, and at that moment, she didn't care if she lived or died herself. Annie was just a kid at the time and maybe it was that detachment from reality that helped her live through the loss. What if it happened again?

I used to think Annie's religion was protective, but now I was afraid that it wasn't enough. Annie had caught her stress cold. She'd had a panic attack. I didn't think she would harm herself, but neither was I sure she would stay out of harm's way.

Annie had said she would visit the casket maker, so I retraced her steps, across Madison and south on 13th. The sky was clear now, but the sun had already dropped below the buildings to the west. The rusty scent of fallen leaves rose from the sidewalk. The front window of the Curiosity Shop cum Casket Store was draped in Halloween-style spider webs. A vintage medical skeleton rested his bony arm on Red Riding Hood's shoulder.

The sandwich sign by the door said the shop would close in 20 minutes. Inside, the young woman, with her slick black hair and red lips, came out from behind an antique cabinet. She wore a green brocade dress dating from the early 1900s but had been cut very short to show off black stockinged legs. I still thought of her as the Goth Girl and put out my hand to introduce myself. "I'm afraid I don't know your name," I said.

"Bebe McCrae," she offered a hand I expected to be manicured with blood red nails, but instead had sensibly clipped nails and callouses.

I was surprised. "Are you the casket maker?" I'd thought of her as a shop girl.

"Learned it from my father and grandfather," she said. "They were disappointed I wasn't a boy." She returned to her place behind the counter to finish a display while we talked. Little glass eyes sparkled in greens and blues made a tinging sound when they hit the bowl. She saw my interest and said, "From the backroom of a doll factory."

"They're fascinating," I said and paused, trying to figure out how to explain my visit. "I haven't heard from my friend, Annie. She told me she was coming here yesterday to see Laurel's apartment."

"God, everyone wants to see the apartment. The police came. They had a search warrant."

I felt the beginnings of a headache and pressed my knuckles into my forehead. A warrant meant they were seriously considering Laurel as a murder suspect. Like Annie, I was afraid they would settle for an easy answer. I vowed to dig deeper. Where was Annie?

"They were in there an hour, but I think they only took stuff like her appointment books." Bebe dropped her voice. "Then her mother came. Again. Laurel's an adult. She needs her distance from parents. I wouldn't let her in."

"Did her father come?"

"No, but I expect he will."

I nodded, wondering if Bebe had parental issues of her own.

"Annie, I would have let Annie in." Her eyes were sad. "You're worried about her, aren't you? Annie is otherworldly. She's carrying too much now. She's struggling." Bebe had expressed my fears exactly.

"So, you saw her."

"No, she hasn't come. It's just that I know things," she said simply. "My work brings me close to death. Sometimes people come to choose their own caskets when they know they are dying, or their loved ones come."

I didn't want to hear Bebe referring to Annie and death together. "Do you sense that something happened to her?"

"I don't know everything." She reached into a cubby in the Victorian desk behind her and pulled out a leather book with designs and photographs of caskets. The photos were black and white, then hand tinted, showing the lovingly crafted wood she'd sanded and carved as if touching the line between this world and the next in her work.

I thought she recognized Annie's otherworldliness because she shared it.

"When Annie was here," Bebe carefully closed her book. "It was as if I could see through her. She was so pale; it was like she was disappearing."

I looked at Bebe's raven hair, her macabre shop filled with antiques and ephemera that recognized the connection between life and death.

"It's nearly Halloween and All Souls." Bebe placed the book back in the desk and smoothed her brocade skirt. "The dead are near, and Annie is not doing well."

"Her aunt died, and the woman was killed out front," I said. I'd felt the same about Annie, though I'd have expressed it differently.

"You'll want to see the apartment, then."

I smiled; with Bebe McCrae I didn't have to put words to my end of the conversation. She knew. We walked outside to the locked door on the street. She used her keys then led up a set of polished wooden stairs to the apartments. The hallway here was wide and airy with an old-fashioned skylight. I evaluated it thinking of Annie's panic—nothing to worry about—but she hadn't been here. Laurel's apartment was the first on the right. Bebe turned her key in the lock and pushed the door open. The apartment was old with box beams and crown molding. The first thing I noticed was beautiful script in deep purple painted on the entry walls. It started at the ceiling and wound to the floor like an art installation. At first. The writing drew me through the archway to the living room. There the newspaper clippings started. Layers upon layers of them. A few weeks earlier it might have been a sign of a project. Now it was a fire hazard. Towers of books, papers and plates with crusted, uneaten food teetered on the desk. I couldn't tell what the police had taken or moved.

"It's not just that the apartment is so crazy. Bad things are happening. A woman murdered, Laurel missing. Annie is missing..." Bebe's eyes showed the same anxiety I felt. "I don't want to leave you here alone. I have to keep the shop open until 5:30."

"The door will be locked."

She didn't budge.

I accepted her foreboding and pulled out my phone. "I'll text my friend with the police department and let him know I'm here. He's usually working on Capitol Hill." I scribbled Nate's number on a scrap of paper and handed it to her as a back-up.

She looked at her watch and nodded. "Fifteen minutes. Then I'll be back." Bebe said and closed the door. The old-fashioned thumb lock on the deadbolt clicked into place.

I couldn't possibly read everything on Laurel's walls. The purple writing listed mental disorders from anorexia, in the entry, to zoophilia in the living room near the desk. There, Laurel had pinned index cards about her family tree, layered on faded photographs, notes and drawings that degenerated into the shag of clippings ripped from newspapers and pages printed from the internet.

I ruffled through the layers, overwhelmed by the volume—an idea of what it was like to be in Laurel's head. The top layer probably reflected her most recent thoughts, so I decided to take pictures to read later. I climbed on a chair and started clicking my phone's camera near the ceiling, working down in columns from left to right. The clock said I had five minutes left, but already I heard a sound at the door. Then the lock turned and clicked.

Chapter 11

Before the door swung open, my thoughts raced. I had to face the possibility that Laurel could be a danger if she'd gone off her medications. Even with my training, I hadn't checked the apartment for an exit plan. I clambered off the chair and straightened my back.

It was Jimmy James who stepped in.

He wore a t-shirt reading Graceful Ox and the straps of his worn backpack pulled his leather jacket askew. He puffed himself up and stood, large and intimidating. "What? You're here?"

I stood tall as well but made myself relax. "I'm worried about Laurel. It's very serious. Haven't the police contacted you? A woman was killed out front. Laurel said she killed her." It was no reason for a mental health evaluator to be in the apartment, but he seemed to accept it.

Jimmy's eyes softened. He lowered his head. I thought his posture lost its threat. Like Bebe, I could usually sense these things, but I was isolated with him in a small space, and I couldn't be sure. He smoothed his already smooth hair and shook his head to negate what I'd said. "I talked to the police. I told them that Laurel's no killer."

"She's very ill. Either ill enough to have killed someone or to believe she had." I wanted him to take Laurel's illness seriously.

He looked around the apartment. "I had no idea," he said. "How could she live like this?"

"You haven't been here?" I asked.

Jimmy shook his head. He was the parent who hadn't experienced Laurel's previous bout of mental illness. He really might not know the seriousness of what she'd been through. Or he still equated treatment with social control.

He left the door and took a few steps toward the tiny kitchen. Cockroaches scurried the instant he came near. The refrigerator door hung open. Still not sure about Jimmy James, I moved toward the apartment door since my exit was no longer blocked.

"I've seen a lot of places like this," I said. "Sometimes people really can't manage. It looks like she wasn't eating."

Plates of untouched takeout food had hardened, and it was impossible to know how long they had been there. Laurel's sheen of competence once she was out of immediate crisis could fool you.

"Really crazy. How do you do this work? Doesn't it get to you?"

"This is my job. It's harder seeing it happen to your child," I said, changing the attention back to him, because I loved my work. I remembered standing in the alcove outside the psych unit at Harborview when both he and Mo were holding on to me. That felt more unsettling than being around people with serious mental illness every day, but I guess that was my problem.

He came back to Laurel's desk and cleared papers from the seat, scooped a heap of draped clothing from the back. He looked for somewhere to place them then just dropped them on the floor. "You think I don't know about mental illness. I do."

I remembered Mo's story about the girl he'd sprung from treatment. I nodded and waited for him to say more.

"There's no way you could know how much experience I have." He put his backpack on the floor and lowered himself to the chair. "I lost my contact with Laurel because I was using heroin." The words and his emotion caught in his throat. "It's why I got clean. Then I remarried and had a son, Jimmy Jr. We called him JJ."

He pulled off his jacket and showed me the tattoo I'd noticed the first time I'd seen him.

"JJ started having problems when he was sixteen. He was into tagging, graffiti." Jimmy Sr. stroked his beard. His face reddened and his eyes filled. I suspected his feelings were always close to the surface. "At first, I thought it was all good, you know, counterculture and artistic. He was angry, then withdrawn. Neither his mother nor I could get him out of his room except to attend school, sometimes not even that." Jimmy hauled himself up to unpin the clipping from the wall and cradled it for me to see. In the picture, a shaved-headed JJ leaned back in a Mick Jagger pose wailing on an electric guitar. He looked vibrantly alive. "This is JJ."

I moved closer. It was an obituary. The initials JJ on his arm weren't self-referential, they were a memorial.

His gaze turned hard. I took a step back.

"My wife and I argued about it. Psychiatrist? Counselor? Medications? She wanted it all. I wanted him to work things through and suggested the counselor. She wanted medications. I understood. People want to act. Medication seems like a quick fix. I said no to all that. More harm than good.

"She agreed to wait, give him a chance to come around. What she didn't tell me was that she took him to our family doctor and got him to prescribe Prozac for depression. Prozac. It has a black box warning for prescribing it to teens. You *know* that!" he accused and stood up. His intensity had returned.

"I know that." I agreed. He was right, teens were at risk for suicide on Prozac, especially within the first few weeks of starting. "The doctor should have done the research."

In the next moment, the apartment door swung and banged against the entry wall startling us both. A police officer, huge in his blues, stepped in. Nate. Bebe stood behind him in the hallway. Finally, realizing I'd been holding my breath, I slowly exhaled.

"Whoa. I'm Laurel's father," Jimmy said, palms up and voice now deferential in the face of authority. "Oh no, is it about Laurel?" A beat later, "Have you found her?"

Nate gave me a questioning look, as if to ask if Jimmy was okay. I gave a subtle shrug. I wasn't sure.

"Ms. McCrae called me. She saw an unauthorized person enter the building." Nate said.

"Oh man, I'm sorry. Jimmy James. We're all looking for Laurel and we're all jumpy, aren't we?"

Bebe stepped into the room. "Where is Laurel?"

"Man, I don't know." Jimmy motioned at the apartment. "I don't think she's been here in a while. I'll be going. Do you think I can keep this?" He showed his son's obituary to Nate but didn't wait for an answer. He turned back to me. "That doctor was a quack." Jimmy's face was flushed, and his eyes were rimmed with red. His voice was barely audible when he said, "JJ committed suicide last October."

"It's just now a year," I said. His anger made sense now. "I'm so sorry."

"And Laurel," he said, his voice drifting off.

I thought about how mental illness ran in his family. Then I thought about my own grandmother. Jimmy and I just had different kinds of denial.

"Medications aren't perfect," I said, "but they can help. Without them, Laurel is in danger too. Is she with you, Jimmy?"

"No and I'm more worried than you are." He still clutched the obituary.

Nate looked at the clipping like he was going to say no but didn't. "You can have it."

Jimmy put it carefully in his wallet and said good-bye.

Bebe watched the hallway until we heard the door to the street close behind him. "I called your policeman friend when I saw the guy let himself in." Bebe folded her arms across her chest and spoke with assurance. "Laurel is with him."

"How do you figure?" Nate asked.

She gave a half smile. "The backpack he was carrying was empty. It was for Laurel's belongings."

I smiled. Bebe was observant. So was I. "At the hospital, he said he didn't have a key to her apartment, but here he was with a key. I guess he's so opposed to treatment that he'd hide her rather than get her back to the hospital."

Bebe locked the door with a key from a jangling metal ring. We followed her downstairs and said good-bye on the sidewalk where Marion Warfield had died.

"Come on down to the car and ride along for a while." Nate's size and warm brown eyes always made me feel everything would be okay, so instead going home, I rode the circuitous route of a beat cop in the big department SUV. The late October dark was falling fast and the air chilled. A fog settled on the neighborhood and dimmed the streetlights and the yellow shop windows.

"Laurel is a prime suspect," he said, confirming what Annie and I had suspected. "That's the conclusion, especially since she's disappeared."

"They need to find her," I said, suddenly irritated that the detectives had made no progress.

"What's the father's address?"

"Our paperwork only had Mom's address. He's from out of town. They might be able to find him through the band he was with. The Graceful Ox."

I told Nate about Annie's reactions to Laurel and all the events that swirled around her, then asked what he thought. The three of us had been through a common experience.

"I never got close to Annie." He spun the steering wheel with his palm, and the radio chattered. "Like I reminded her of the shooting. It was too hard."

"Exactly," I said and filled him in on her panic attack at work. "Now, I can't get ahold of her. I'm worried."

"She might be stronger than you think, in spite of this mess."

Said the man who never got close to Annie. I wished I could be reassured so easily.

The ride calmed me. We cruised north from Cal Anderson Park that capped the old Broadway Reservoir, up to Lakeshore Boulevard, then Nate circled back onto Broadway. A line of red taillights snaked down to the stop light at Republican. The Honda in front of us had a brake light out and Nate tapped its license number into the computer attached to his dashboard. "Don't ever drive with a broken light," he said. "We'll run your tabs to find out if you're driving a stolen car."

"I'll remember that." I said, then grabbed my phone to find the note I'd made when Nell and I did the All-Home Count. "Can you run this one? This guy was watching Mo James' restaurant in the middle of the night."

Nate entered the number. "Registered in Skagit County to a guy named Theodore Martinez."

"Anything else?" I asked.

He touched the computer. "This shows every contact he's had with police." He waited until the next stop light to squint at the information on the screen. "An illegal right turn on red. A call to 911 about some neighbors. He's had an arrest, but it was before everything was computerized."

"Is there a way to find out?" My thoughts cleared. Laurel's family was troubled enough to make me wonder if Martinez could have something to do with the murder.

"Not in this data base. I'll look when I'm back at the station."

Nate drove me back to Annie's apartment. Her windows were lit dimly, and she still didn't pick up her phone. She'd told me she was scheduled to work this evening, so while we idled in front of her apartment, I called the office. What I learned wasn't good. Annie had been a no show at the afternoon meeting. No sick call, she just never showed up. When I checked my messages, they were filled with calls from my colleagues wondering if I'd heard from her and if she was alright.

Chapter 12

Annie was responsible, not the type who didn't show up for work without calling. My fears went through the roof. Had Annie been stressed enough to harm herself? Was Laurel more dangerous than she'd thought? Or had someone else harmed her when she set out to prove Laurel innocent of murder. I talked Nate into coming along while I tried to get into Annie's apartment to check. I'd met Megan, the apartment manager before. She was an artist who lived in the lower, right hand unit. It was all lit up, so we aimed pebbles at her window until she lifted the sash. Her always messy hair had been dyed pink and pulled back into a bun. I gave her the brief story of my concerns and asked if we could check the apartment. Having Nate there added gravity to my request.

"Annie's friend, I remember you," Megan said when she met us at the door wearing paint splattered jeans and flannel shirt. We followed her up the stairs to the second floor.

I knocked on the dark paneled door and called Annie's name. First quietly then louder. No answer, but loud enough for the neighbor across the hall to open his door and confirm that he hadn't seen Annie either.

Megan unlocked the door and Nate protectively stepped in first. I looked around him. The apartment wasn't big, just one bedroom and the big living room/dining room. It only took a second to see that it was empty. In the kitchen, the dragon bowls we'd used for pho were unwashed, but neatly stacked in the sink. In the bedroom, the bed was made.

Nate pulled the closet open and checked under the bed. "Looking for suitcases," he said. We saw a crumpled duffel, but it didn't seem to prove anything, except that we didn't know where Annie could be.

I checked my watch. It was after 7:30. I knew she usually went to the Sunday evening Mass at Seattle University. In her current state she might miss work, but I didn't think she'd skip that. If I hurried, I could be there on time.

Annie had brought me to the St. Ignatius Chapel when it was first built, a jewel on the campus at the Jesuit University. The spare, modern building had baffles and sails to catch the light, but in late October, the sun was down long before the 8:00 service. I passed a reflecting pool that mirrored the lit windows and pulled open a tall cedar door.

I expected students, but people of all ages and nationalities filled the entrance. The crowd was stuck on a gentle incline that led to the font where people dipped their fingers into the holy water and crossed themselves, but a glass display case was the cause of the bottleneck.

I felt a hand on my shoulder and turned to see one of the chaplains from Harborview, a small-boned Black man who looked impossibly young to be giving advice of the soul, but according to Annie, was old beyond his years in spiritual wisdom. "I recognize you from the hospital," he said. "Welcome. You'll find it busier than usual tonight."

"I'm glad to see a familiar face," I said, scanning the crowd. "You know Annie Bartoz. I'm looking for her."

"I haven't seen her but have a look around. She comes every week. Did you know Marion?"

My heart stopped as I realized that this was not the usual Sunday evening Mass. "Marion Warfield?"

"You didn't know? After the service tonight there's a recognition of her life. We don't know how long until there can be a funeral. She's been such a big part of the community. Her death was shocking." He motioned to the crowd. "You can tell how gifted Marion was. She touched a lot of people."

The strangeness shook me. I came looking for Annie but wandered into a memorial for the woman who'd been murdered instead. Now when I looked at the crowd, I felt a buzz of uneasiness, as if people's muted conversations weren't just honoring Marion, they were wondering how safe they were. I wondered if Annie had known Marion Warfield more than she'd told me. This community didn't look that big.

"I'm so sorry," I told the chaplain, looking into his brown eyes hoping for information if not wisdom. "I heard Marion Warfield was brilliant, but we never met. Did Annie know her?"

The crowd inched us forward. From here, I could see the simple altar. Even after dark, the chapel walls reflected greens and yellows on their roughened plaster. "Of course, she did," he answered. "They served on the student liturgy committee together." Annie's denial of knowing the dead woman added to my confusion.

All the people in somber clothing moving toward the glass cases gave me a moment of claustrophobia. If Annie hadn't told the truth about knowing Marion Warfield, she'd probably held back more. We finally reached the memorabilia: books and photographs of her in groups of students where she looked like a warm, professional presence, so unlike the ripped and heavily made-up woman Nate had described.

"Was Marion..." I struggled to frame a question about a private life that clashed with the public presence. "A police officer told me she was dressed, um, kind of like a demon. Ripped stockings and bizarre make-up."

The chaplain folded his hands before answering, "It's nearly Halloween."

"She had just left a therapy session; a client could have seen her."

It took a few beats for him to answer. "Brokenness was Marion's gift. Her troubles brought her to God."

"What..."

The chaplain must have interpreted my reaction as sadness. He touched my arm. "Some people give more after death," he gestured to the alter and the crucifix with Jesus on the cross, his head hanging, lifeless. The metaphor of the greatest martyr of Western civilization was not as comforting as he meant it to be.

Piano chords started from the front of the chapel, a requiem. A student approached the chaplain and led him away to other duties. I found a seat along the back wall so I could watch for Annie.

The music swelled and the priest, who looked like a football player in green robes, processed in. He gave his blessing and read from the gospel, "They brought to him all who were ill or possessed by demons. He cured many and drove out many demons."

I cradled my head in my hands, tired of the demon image that seemed to be following me.

The priest's theme turned out to be woundedness. "We need to feel our wounds, not just think ourselves out of them." His words seemed directed to me. It was the reason I gravitated to crisis work—I wasn't all that comfortable with the feeling part. I just wanted problems I could assess and decisions I could make. Looking around the chapel made me realize I didn't like the idea of God being in charge either. I wanted to handle things myself.

The homily moved on to other demons when a tall man entered the chapel. He was dressed in black: black jeans and Doc Martins; a black sweater and raincoat even though it wasn't raining. He had the look of a Roman god, with an aquiline nose and tousled curls. In a room filled with polite sadness, he seemed truly distressed. He paced at the back of the chapel then stopped, centered in the aisle leading to the altar. One by one, parishioners turned to evaluate his demeanor which had started as restlessness and kindled into anger.

"Rest in Peace. Rip and rend." He muttered. The volume of his words increased in a crescendo.

More heads turned, and people whispered. They were uncomfortable. As always, I was drawn to handling the situation when someone needed calming. I glanced around the room, but no one official was responding, so I stood and joined him. The man was walking again, and I matched my speed to his. "I'm so sorry. Do you want to talk in the vestibule?"

He didn't respond but followed when I led the way back to the photographs.

We looked at the clippings and pictures and his body seemed to vibrate with such agony that even standing near him was painful. He ran his hands over his face. That's when I saw the resemblance between the woman in the photographs and the man in black. "Marion was your sister," I whispered.

"Yes," he said so quietly I had to lean in to hear.

I touched his arm and introduced myself, normally I would explain my connection to the deceased, but not today. "What is your name?"

"Emery Warfield." He pulled at his clothes as if he truly wanted to rend them in Old Testament grief. "We were twins."

The thought of Marion and Emery together since the womb made his loss larger. I had no words to comfort him, so I just kept physical contact, holding on to his arm that shuddered with pain.

After moment, Emery spoke. "They don't know her." A large backpack, also black, rested against the display case. He touched it protectively. I must have looked surprised to see that he carried his belongings with him. "It's mine. You think that I don't look homeless? None of us are what we seem."

"What happened?"

He knelt by his backpack and unzipped the main compartment. "Evicted for an argument with my landlord. I couldn't sleep on people's couches forever, not even Marion's. Once you are on the streets, it's impossible to climb out." He lifted a shaving kit and placed it on the floor. Underneath was an envelope protected in a plastic bag. "Three times my phone was stolen. No one could call to tell me Marion died. A cousin found me where I camp. He brought me this."

Emery Warfield slowly removed the protective wrap. He passed me an envelope.

I opened it reverently to find photographs of a young Marion. I searched her now-familiar face for a clue to what led to her death. "She was beautiful," I murmured and turned to the next photo, a teenaged Marion and Emery boating on a sparkling lake ringed by Douglas fir, with a once grand white house in the background. I recognized it as the Adolescent Center in Burien where Annie had worked. I set aside a rising anger at Annie for knowing much more about Marion Warfield than she'd told me and wondered how troubled Marion Warfield had been, had continued to be. The brokenness the chaplain mentioned might have led to her death if she had been inappropriate with her clients.

"You were both beautiful," I said, turning my attention back to her brother. "How could this happen?" The questions were unanswerable. A simple chain of events couldn't explain what lead to his homelessness or her death. I glanced back to the chapel. "Some people would blame God."

Emery rocked almost imperceptibly. "Not Marion," he said. "She'd say this would have happened a long time ago without God."

I started to ask how, but at the same moment, bells chimed from his pocket.

He pulled out a smart phone in a pearlized case. Apparently, Emery had a new phone, if not an apartment. He said hello, listened without speaking, then turned it off. He took the photographs from my hand, wrapped, and returned them to his backpack and swung it onto his shoulder. He paused to steel himself. "I'm going," he said and strode out the door.

Inside the chapel, the priest still spoke. Instead of going back in, I hurried outside after Emery, hoping I hadn't lost him. But the walkways were deserted. No sign of a man in black. No sounds but the gentle lap of the water against the wall of the reflecting pool, young voices talking across campus and a car accelerating on 12th Avenue.

I returned to the vestibule while Mass droned on. By the glass case, visitors had written tributes in a beautifully bound book. One caught my eye.

Marion Warfield was my teacher. She humbly told us all she remembered about her own mental illness—the only person I know who didn't hide behind normalcy. Marion gave me hope.

Religion clearly meant a lot to Marion Warfield, but it wasn't what helped me. I left before Mass ended to go to the altar of the Bourbon Bar. There was nowhere else to look for Annie, so I was looking for Laurel again, wondering if Laurel was a danger to others or if she was in danger too. Wondering if this search had led Annie into trouble too.

The Columbia City Theater couldn't have looked more different than the sleepy late-night bar I visited a few days ago. On the sidewalk, a hellish wall of cigarette smoke rose and curled from a dozen black clad revelers at the door. Variations of dragons and daggers dripping with blood had been silkscreened on the backs of black leather jackets and the fronts of black tee shirts. Uncombed black hair topped most heads. Only one young woman was beautifully groomed and wearing a blue cape and mini skirt that might have been appropriate anywhere, but her bare legs marked her to fit in: tattoos like a medieval dream climbed up a net of color—like Nell's art books. It seemed redundant, but Marion Warfield would have fit in here.

I looked down at my silver quilted jacket and faded blue jeans and felt ultra conservative. Had I known; I could have come in something more fitting. Black was a Northwest wardrobe staple—I had plenty. Ingnoring my clothes, I waded through the smoke to get to the door.

The door said the theater was closed on Sundays, but a poster marked this as a special event. Festival of Evil—a showcase for rising metal groups with names like Torture Rack, Blood and Blaspherian. It was running on the Sundays and Mondays bracketing Halloween. The bouncer at the door took one look at me and recommended I try a bar down the street for a drink, but I told him I was meeting someone. Laurel's father said he was sitting in with different bands, maybe metal was included.

The music was loud, and the room smelled of stale beer and cigarette smoke that clung to the concert goers' clothing when they came inside. I didn't see Jimmy James anywhere. I did see the redheaded bartender and the man with the mutton chop sideburns who had downed my bourbon the last time. He had changed to all black of course, but mostly he just looked drunk. I joined him and resisted the urge to take his glass in retribution.

"Different crowd," I commented. "I may not find Jimmy James tonight."

The man took the last sip of his drink and tapped his glass on the bar to get the server's attention. He put up two fingers and pointed to me.

"I owe you a drink," he said.

"You remember?"

"I admit I'm drunk, but I have an excellent memory," he slurred. "Jimmy loves this crowd. He was playing with Antichrist but left early. You still looking for his daughter?"

I nodded.

"I think he's gone home. He was freaking agitated—which fits with the crowd, but I think it was cause his favorite girl didn't show up tonight. He was crazy about her."

"I missed him." I said, deflated. "Interesting crowd. Did you notice the woman with the tattoos climbing her legs?"

"Oh sure. There are two types here: the real rockers and the ones with the tats that they can cover up tomorrow when they go back to their work-a-day world." He picked up his empty glass and slid his tongue down the side in a gesture that looked obscene. Mostly he seemed impatient to get his new drink. "Jimmy's rocker girl has some outstanding tats on her shoulders. A nice blue that goes with a black dress. I told you Jimmy likes projects, but he has an excellent nose for potential—women who will be willing and able to support him, 'cause he doesn't work much. There's no money in this."

He waved at the music venue. The bartender arrived and wiped the counter with a rag. She finally set down the fresh drinks. He smiled.

"Mo had potential." I reflected and took a sip of my bourbon.

"Obviously. She was in the restaurant biz from the time she was fourteen. Worked under the table, lied about her age. She was always good with food."

"You've known Jimmy and Mo that long."

"Since the beginning. It was the '80s, there were empty buildings downtown, and everybody shared everything. Food, places to stay, girls." He gave a smile that suggested he had shared Mo.

"Youth…" I replied just to keep him going.

"I hate how Seattle has become a playground for techies. They tear down anything with human history to put in two soulless boxes."

"Amazon and Google are the real devil." I waved my hand to rule out the crowd in black. The bourbon and lack of sleep were going to my head.

"You've got it sister."

I sat up straighter and took a pull on the bourbon. I needed to find Laurel. "Too bad I missed Jimmy. Do you have his phone number?"

"No. I don't set up gigs, so I have no reason to call him."

I slumped again. There was no reason not to tell the guy my fears. "I'm afraid his daughter is with him. He's that opposed to the mental health system."

"You probably didn't get the memo that most people hate a system that locks folks up."

"Some do," I agreed, "but a lot of parents are so worried about their sick kids that they are relieved to have the system."

His head nodded to his chest. I'd put him to sleep. I pulled my coat from the bar stool and slipped in an arm before feeling a tug on the coat that prevented me from continuing.

"You can find him at 'Stended Stay." He slurred.

"What?"

"Ex-tended Stay down by the airport." He enunciated the syllables this time.

"The apartment hotel?"

"Cheapest place in town. He stayed in room 320. I remember. Called it 320 Land of Plenty."

Chapter 13

The Bourbon Bar again made me tired. I opened my window crossing the bridge into Duvall and let the cold night air keep me awake for the last leg of my journey.

Behind in town, there were no more streetlights. The slice of sky between the towering evergreens on either side of the road was black and starless.

Our windows glowed yellow when I pulled up. Caesar pressed his nose against the mullioned front door and circled me with joy when I stepped in. Frank and Nell lounged on the couch, watching a movie, and paused it, freezing a close-up of a young Juliette Binoche.

"Finally," Frank said. "I can't believe you're still standing." He followed me to the kitchen to get a snack.

"How's Nell?" I whispered so she couldn't hear her concerned parents evaluating her mood. I'd called home to check in with her, but that wasn't the same.

"She talked at dinner. This thing has sent her into a tailspin about her career. She thought she'd found her calling, but now she feels like an outsider." He poured me a glass of Spanish Tempranillo while I made enough paper-thin slices of the Manchego cheese for all of us. We'd gotten these in honor of Nell's trip preparations. "I think she's worn out for now, but you should spend more time with her tomorrow."

I couldn't tell if he was passing the torch or trying to make me feel guilty for spending the day in the city but decided not to press the issue. "Is the movie helping?" I asked, picking up the plate to head back to the living room.

Frank nodded.

Caesar stayed close, not letting me out of his sight, but I knew it was the food, not my presence he was concerned about.

"What are you watching?" I passed Nell a piece of cheese and sank onto the couch next to her.

"Chocolat," Nell answered. "An oldie. I thought it would get me in the mood for visiting Gwen in France.

I plucked the Manchego from her hand. "You'll want Brie then."

She grabbed it back and smiled. "Juliette Binoche comes to this rigid little town to open a chocolate shop and she knows which candy will arouse each person's deepest desires." She clicked the remote to start it again and the camera followed stone streets and medieval buildings to a beauty salon with 1950s hair dryers where women gossiped about change.

"I saw this. It's like a fairytale." I sipped my wine and watched as the chocolate shop became a haven for misfits and Juliette instructed a woman in the making of truffles. The chocolate was so rich and shiny I thought I could smell it. After a minute, I was dying for dessert. "Do we have any chocolate?" I asked.

"No chocolate," Frank said sadly.

"Oh yes," Nell answered. "We have that good cocoa left from cookie baking. How long would it take to whip up those chocolate cookies?" She paused the movie again and we padded back to the kitchen in our stocking feet.

"Sounds great," Frank said and flipped to the news. Maybe he had been passing the torch.

I rummaged around in the open pantry shelves my grandfather had built by the back door. I found the flour and sugar and baking powder and put them on the table for mixing while Nell pulled eggs and butter from the refrigerator. The bitter aroma of burnt earth rose from the cocoa. I got stuck by the back door, with the feeling I'd had that morning, of some memory if only I could find it. A wave of exhaustion hit.

I leaned against the wall, and the memory came closer. When I was a girl and I stayed with my grandparents for the summer, I used to sit under the table where it always seemed cool. It was my sanctuary. I stayed for hours, making up stories and playing with treasures I saved in a foil clad chocolate candy box. A box I'd saved when I cleared out these shelves of the mouse droppings and detritus that accumulated in my grandparents old age.

"Mom," Nell's voice seemed to be coming from very far away. "Are you okay?"

Caesar nosed me. I shook my head to clear it. "I was just so tired there for a minute." I saw that she had already mixed the eggs and sugar and had the dry ingredients ready for the cocoa still clutched in my hand.

"Maybe you should go to bed. You're going to make yourself sick," she said and took the packet.

"I'm wide awake now. I'll sleep fine tonight." I turned to the shelves and pushed canned tomatoes and boxes of pasta aside without luck. Then a stack of bowls and a basket of dishtowels. I shuddered at how dusty things had become. Finally, I found the yellow candy box with my childhood treasures. "Look," I called to Nell, but she was intent on her work. She had rolled out the dough and pressed cookie cutters into the chocolaty sheet, then lifted it off leaving behind chocolate forest animals on the wooden board. I set the candy box aside and made a simple frosting. When the cookies were in the oven, the warm smell of chocolate transformed the house into something like a French town.

I showed the candy box to Nell while we waited. "Remember this?"

She took it and ran her fingers over the raised letters and bright tulips that decorated the lid then pulled it off to reveal feathers, empty wooden spools, and tiny dolls I'd made from scraps. It was so old fashioned like it was from an era before my own childhood. "Your treasure box."

"More than that," I said. "It's a box from Van der Meer's candies in Mount Vernon, Washington. That's where Mom lived before her real mother died. The chocolate makers were her neighbors. I remember them."

"You think they might know something about Grandma Rose's mother going to Northern State."

"Maybe." I remembered going there to visit with Mom. They were a Dutch couple with a yellow brick storefront.

Nell plated the cookies to carry back to the living room where we curled up on the couch and watched Juliette Binoche transform a hide bound French village with chocolate. Our own concoction melted on our tongues. I fell asleep before the movie ended.

I should have been able to sleep late the next morning, but my thoughts woke me. Laurel and Annie. I tried and failed to reach Annie. Again, I didn't know what else to do.

I had a string of days off, so I pulled on my clothes, left Frank warm in bed and went out to Nell's cottage. She was awake but still in bed. The springs creaked when I sat down beside her. "Want to take a road trip?" I was restless, feeling helpless about finding Annie and guilty about neglecting Nell, especially since the incident with her boss.

Nell pulled the covers over her head. "When?"

"Right now."

"Where?"

"First, I want to go to Tukwila." I explained 'Stended Stay and that I thought Laurel was with Jimmy James.

She moaned and lowered the quilt to her nose, her hair scrunched into a rats nest on the side that was still longer. "And second?"

"Mount Vernon."

"You're looking for the Van Der Meers. They've probably been gone for years."

"Third, we can go to what's left of Northern State Hospital in Sedro Wooley. Unless I hear from Annie. Then we turn around."

Nell sat up in bed and pulled the covers around her. "That might be interesting."

"It'll do us both good," I said.

"Only if we can spend the night," Nell said. "That would be fun."

We went up to the kitchen to plan. Nell brought my mom's diaries and ate deer shaped cookies while she looked for sections about Mount Vernon, but that was before she'd started documenting her days.

Frank got up when he smelled the coffee. We filled him in on the plan.

"Good idea," he whispered when Nell went to get her computer to find a place to stay. "But you might not find a thing."

"It doesn't matter," I said. "I read that they turned the hospital's old dairy farm into a park. We can take a walk."

"Take Caesar with you then." Frank said.

"Okay." I wasn't sure if he wanted Caesar to have a good romp, or for Nell and me to have a dog who could be protective. Both were fine with me.

"Yes." Nell was back and grabbed a container to fill with dog food for the trip. I went upstairs to pack a change of clothes. We didn't manage to get on the road until noon.

When I pulled out of the driveway, Nell pulled her feet up onto the car seat and hugged her knees. She wasn't wearing any make-up, but the buzzed side of her head and, now that she'd combed it out, the longer swoop of hair on the other side looked perfect.

"Stended Stay here we come," she said.

The Extended Stay was an apartment-hotel chain nestled in a concrete elbow of land between I-5 and Route 518 to SeaTac airport. It was the kind of place you'd find in any city and pass a million times and without giving a second look. Beyond the faux-stone pillars stood the basic motel. I realized that if I did find Laurel, I'd just sabotaged the first part of our trip. We would have to wait for the police to arrive. Then I'd probably have to deal with an outraged Jimmy James. Bad idea. Nell agreed to wait in the car for this part.

Inside, despite the striped carpet and terracotta accent wall, the ceilings were low and the lighting dim. Instant claustrophobia.

"Can I help you?" The young desk clerk had blown-out brown hair and a blue suit jacket that made me think she was hoping to move up the road to the airport and become a flight attendant.

"Meeting a friend upstairs," I answered. She seemed satisfied with my answer, but still watched me make my way to the elevators, taking her job of minding the lobby seriously. I pushed 3. The elevator doors opened to a stark hallway that ran in either direction with identical doors. *320 Land of Plenty*, as Jimmy had called it, was to the left.

I thought about Laurel's aging-musician father with the tattoo honoring his dead son. He sat in with different bands. Maybe he was a good musician, but he wasn't making money. I always pictured people like that staying with friends in shabby shared houses. Had Seattle's new development and prices pushed those out too? I would have preferred an overcrowded house to Extended Stay's bland flavors. Every door I passed seemed to have a TV blaring inside.

The door to 320 was open and a vacuum cleaner hummed inside. I expected to see the advertised weekly cleaning in progress, instead, the room had been wiped clean of personal belongings. Jimmy James was gone. I'd missed him. The cleaner, a large woman with a t-shirt that read BRAZIL stretched across her breasts, made zig zag vacuum stripes in the blue carpet. If Jimmy was gone, Laurel was gone too.

"I'm looking for the man who stayed here. I guess he checked out."

"Gone," the cleaning woman turned off the vacuum and echoed my thoughts in a Portuguese tinted accent. "No tip and a lot of garbage." Her cart was heaped with black plastic bags.

"Did you see him with his daughter? A young woman?"

"More than one young women," she answered with a knowing nod.

The door to the next apartment opened a few inches and the resident, a 40ish woman in tight jeans and tattooed eyebrows on a worn face, wedged her body in the space. "Walls are thin here," she scowled. The lights hummed overhead.

"What did you hear?" I asked, hoping for information.

"I heard you, lady. Asking questions about things that are none of your business. These are our homes, okay? Just because it sounds temporary it's what we've got. Would you go nosing around house cleaners in Mercer Island?"

Under the circumstances, I would, but held my words.

"Respect our privacy." She demanded and stared at me with a look designed to make me turn and head back to the elevators. However, I stayed, and it paid off. She wanted privacy but couldn't stop herself from talking and talking. "People are always coming around here thinking they have a right to walk in. Jimmy James was a good man. He wasn't here long. He lives in California. He got music gigs here. Sure, he had a lot of women who visited, but that stopped as soon as his daughter came to stay. She's a great kid. I know she can conquer the world because she's a storyteller. She has stories she is searching for and stories she's telling. A writer. A girl like her can take the sun and shine it on her topic and the waters will rise like mists. She won't have to walk on water, she'll move the water and move mountains too. Like Moses."

She talked so fast that I guessed she had a psychiatric diagnosis too. Getting a word in would have been like jumping in front of a train, but I was excited to learn that Laurel had been here and confiding in the woman. I took the chance, "What stories?"

It was a bad call. The woman huffed back into her apartment and slammed the door. Her words didn't stop, but I couldn't hear them distinctly enough to understand. I waited a few minutes, but she didn't come back to the hallway, so I headed downstairs and stopped by the desk where the young clerk was on the phone giving information about apartments. I wasn't sure why, but I stood patiently while she explained that they had few rooms because a block was reserved for homeless families with motel vouchers. Extended Stay was earning a warmer place in my heart. Finally, the woman in the blue blazer hung up.

"I was supposed to meet the man in 320," I said, "Jimmy James, but it seems he's moved on."

"Right!" She chirped. "He left this morning. Said he got a gig playing with a band up in Conway. In the Pub. You know it?"

I shook my head, no.

"It's up near La Connor. I go with my boyfriend on the weekends. He's into Ducati." She read the confusion on my face and answered my unasked question. "The Italian Motorcycle? All different bike clubs meet up at the Conway Pub. I'm going to hear him play on my day off."

The BRAZIL-shirted housekeeper pulled out of the next elevator and left the cart parked in a side hall and told the woman at the desk she'd be taking her break.

"Oh, in the Skagit Valley. Maybe I'll check it out." I thanked her and found myself imagining her changing from her blazer and wondering if she had any of the discretely covered tattoos like the women at the bar last night. Perhaps a lot of women had a secret beyond the image they showed during the day.

A flashing light on the desk phone drew her attention. I mouthed a thank you and moved toward the door but decided to check my messages before leaving. Nothing. I perched for a moment on an upholstered bench by the door and tried Annie's number, by now a useless ritual.

The desk clerk hung up the phone and left her post at the counter. In that moment, I realized I was all alone with the cleaning cart and the black bags of garbage from Jimmy's room. Even if I found nothing more than crumpled tissues and a dried-up toothpaste, it was Jimmy's secret world. I wanted to see it, probably the same impulse that led me into mental health. I wanted to get to the bottom of things.

Fortunately, a box of nitrile gloves was tucked in with the supplies on the cleaning cart. Knowing I didn't have long for my search, I pulled on a pair and checked the top bag. Nothing but coffee grounds and candy bar wrappers: Milky Way to Three Musketeers. Jimmy James' diet was not healthy. The second bag had more kitchen waste and a rotting smell that made me breathe through my mouth. Banana peels and apple cores gave me more hope for his health. The third bag was pay dirt. I found long strips of the white gauze that had dressed Laurel's wrists. And papers. Millions of crumpled papers filled with the same handwriting I'd seen in her apartment. I grabbed some extra gloves and made a speedy exit though the double glass doors with the garbage bag—all before the clerk or the cleaner returned.

Chapter 14

Low clouds darkened the sky. Nell and I took turns driving north from the Extended Stay. Caesar snored in the backseat. By the time we reached Conway, where Jimmy James would be playing, sheets of rain swept across the fields of stubble. It was too early for music; we'd have to circle back for Jimmy in the evening. Now I was certain he was harboring Laurel.

Mount Vernon was up the road. When we arrived, the rain let up, but the town was draped in clouds. The Skagit River and its waterfront park ran beside a grid of brick-faced shops built in the early 1900s. We took Caesar for a walk beside the river where the waters ran fast.

I told Nell I would recognize where the chocolate shop had been because I had learned how to read there. The building had its name and date in raised concrete letters between the second story windows. U-n-i-o-n, I remember sounding it out and the year it was built, 1908. Why I expected to find a chocolate shop that had been there in the 70's, the only time my mother brought me to visit, I'd never know. Instead of a chocolate shop, we found a gluten free bakery called Shambala. I told Nell that walking in the footsteps of those who'd gone before was probably all we'd get. I'd had great hopes of a revelation, but whenever I visited a place with history, I only saw the empty space where battles had occurred—either historic or family.

Nell wouldn't tolerate my self-pity. "I need a treat anyway," she said and pulled me across the wet sidewalk and through the door like she used to when she was little.

I looked around with a lump in my throat. The glass display case was the same. The smell wasn't far off, but the milk chocolate was overlaid with baking bread. The rest was all black ceiling, white walls, and bright paintings. An upright piano and a sofa covered in red velvet backed the room. I liked it but it wasn't what I was looking for. I wanted to see the same café tables I remembered.

Baked goods filled the old glass case: glazed cinnamon rolls, fruit tarts, and stacks of cookies from chocolate chip to sugar to molasses. The man behind the counter was about thirty with plugs in his earlobes and a crocheted rainbow hat on a mountain of brown hair. "Can I help you?" he asked.

I stared helplessly at the baked goods. "It looks good, but I actually came in because I remembered this as a candy store from when I was a kid."

"Van Der Meer's." His voice was kind and buttery warm.

"Yes. But you're too young remember it."

"My grandma is a Van Der Meer."

"I wonder if she remembers our family," Nell said. "They were friends."

"Want to find out? Come sit down. I'll get you some tea and a pastry." He led us to a table and helped us off with our coats, hanging them on a rack near the door. When he returned, he whispered, "I'll call. She lives upstairs," then loudly when she came on the phone, "Grandma, there are two ladies here to see you," a pause then, "What's your family name?"

"Cooper," I said, a name I'd never heard used because my grandparents had adopted my mother and given her their name.

"She'll be down in a minute. I'll bring you something to eat," he said and disappeared without asking us what we wanted. In less than a minute, he was back with a fragrant pot of tea and two desserts he placed with a flourish. "It's on the house—Chocolate Mousse Pie and Chocolate Peach Tart—I knew you would want the chocolate because you remembered the candy store." Then he disappeared to help a customer at the counter.

Nell took a bite of the mousse pie and leaned across the table, "It's like the movie—he knows which dessert I was longing for."

I tried the tart with glistening peaches drizzled with chocolate and believed it. He knew. Before my second bite, the front door opened, and a white-haired woman hobbled in clutching the arm of a young woman helper with one hand and wielding a cane with the other. She could barely walk but she wore a pair of four-inch silver heels that brought her height to almost five feet. I smiled automatically and she beamed in return. I went to meet her and bent over to give her a hug. Both her name and images of the day I met her came flooding back. "Auntie Iris, I remember you!"

"Little Gracie" She said with no sense of irony. With her white hair and blue eyes, she looked like a tiny Dutch grandmother doll. "You haven't changed a bit." She handed me her cane with the assumption that I would secure her other arm on the walk to the table.

Nell stood up to be introduced, then took Iris' hand when we all sat down. "Those are some shoes," she said.

"Jon is my great grandson," she said nodding to the rainbow hatted man. "He tells me they are frivolous. It just shows how little people understand about what makes a person feel good. These shoes are worth every wobble, but I only wear them on special occasions."

Jon arrived and poured her a cup of tea and brought her a lavender scented short bread.

"He knows my favorite," Iris said. "Now tell me about your family. This must be your daughter."

I introduced Nell and found myself speechless. What could I tell her about my mother? Not her depression. There was so much more to my mother than that, but I always got stuck there.

Iris saved me by telling me stories instead. "Your mother, Rose, and I were best friends. We did everything together. We dressed the same. We played dolls. We took piano lessons together. I didn't have a piano, so I practiced at your mother's house. She was my best friend until she moved away when we were nine or ten. We wrote letters, but she rarely came back." Now Iris was caught in the silence.

Nell took over, sensing the difficulty. "That's the reason we came. Grandma Rose died this year."

Iris' face was all sympathy. "I'm sorry dear."

"Thank you," Nell said. "We found the diaries she kept all her life. I read about you, and the piano lessons. That's when she started writing."

"Music ran in Rose's family. Her mother played by ear and entertained at all the parties."

"What songs did she play?" I hadn't heard many stories about this grandmother and liked knowing about her music.

"I liked *Some Enchanted Evening,* and all the grownups slow dancing." Iris' eyelids fluttered with the memory.

"What we didn't know was anything about her mother's mental illness," Nell said. "That was why she moved away. Do you remember anything?"

Iris pursed her lips as her favorite memory slipped away. "Her mother went to the hospital and died. That's why she moved."

"I wonder what happened to the piano," I said looking at the old upright.

"That's not it," Iris pointed a jeweled hand accusingly across the room. "One day I went to Rose's house and the piano was dismantled. At first, I just thought it was broken, but Rose was crying and said her mother did it—looking for the ghosts. That's when the piano lessons ended." She turned her teacup around and around, disturbed. She studied the flowered cup that didn't match our simple restaurant crockery. "We loved flowers because of our names. I still do." She took a careful sip and was at a loss for words.

"Did her mother do anything else unusual?" I asked, even though I knew Iris wouldn't tell me. Her warmth chilled. I decided to reveal more about myself, hoping she would too. "Rose—my mother—suffered from depression, so I wondered about what happened. Things that affected her. She didn't talk about it."

"Exactly," she leaned forward and spoke in a firm voice. "I didn't ask, she didn't tell. It's not right to upset people by mentioning it."

"I know. People don't discuss mental illness even now, less so then. There's shame and embarrassment. Did the adults say anything about it? Anything that would give me a clue about what happened?"

"Of course not. That wouldn't be talk for a child to hear. And that's why Rose never wanted you to know. We want everything to be nice for children."

"Of course, we aren't children anymore." I bristled and tried to think of another way to ask, since obviously, everything wasn't nice for a girl whose mother was looking for ghosts in the piano. I wondered if those ghosts had led to my life-long preoccupation with mental health.

Iris broke in before I formulated my next questions. "It was better that Rose live with a new family and have a normal life. These days everyone wants to go on TV with their problems. I don't agree with that."

I glanced at Nell who had been watching the volley between Iris and me. Her face was calm and accepting of the impasse. The beautiful tart sat, untouched since my first bite. My desires were being seriously frustrated here. A mixture of sadness and frustration flooded me. "I understand about privacy, but Mom is dead now. I've worked in mental health all my life and it can help to know..."

Iris cut me off, setting her cup down in its saucer with a clatter. "You're like my sister, Lily, always digging. She worked with those people up in Sedro Wooley until it closed. We called it the bug house."

"She worked at Northern State Hospital?"

"Oh yes. She was a nurse. Those people should be kept apart like they were in the old days. I don't want them next door. Down in Seattle the crazy people are on every corner."

Her attitude made me feel like crying. I knew that stigma was alive and well but didn't expect to hear her biases expressed so hurtfully.

"Is Lily still alive?" Nell asked.

"She's still up there. The hospital has been closed for years but she won't let it go. She's worried about the graves."

"The patient's graves?" Nell and I spoke at the same time.

"Maybe we could talk to her," I said.

"Let it go, young ladies." Iris turned in her chair and grabbed her cane.

Had she been able, she would have gotten up and stormed away, but her feel-good shoes were an impediment. No matter how bad she made me feel, I decided to take the high road and stood. "Thank you so much for talking to us, Auntie Iris. Nell and I have another stop to make, so we'll be going."

Her caregiver helped her to the door.

Nell and I left the half-eaten desserts on the table and gathered our coats. Then I remembered my manners and went to the counter to thank the rainbow-hatted man for his hospitality and well-intentioned sweets. He did have the Juliette Binoche thing down. He packed the desserts in white boxes and met my every desire by slipping a napkin with Lily Van der Meer's phone number into my hand.

I dialed as soon as we were outside. The other Van Der Meer sister took my grandmother's name and arranged to see us in the morning. Then, because the rain had let up, Nell and I walked Caesar by the river until it was time to go looking for Jimmy and Laurel again.

The woman in Extended Stay had regaled me with stories of the Conway Pub, the bikers and oyster burgers. There weren't many Harleys, Hondas, and Ducati's on a Monday, but we still had to park down the block. The tall white building with its hipped roof dominated the tiny business district. The Dutch style fit the tulip madness that dominated the Skagit Valley each spring. Inside, the crowd was sparse except for a few locals playing pull tabs at the bar. Nell and I took a seat at one of the long tables and watched Jimmy warm up with his current musical partners. This was a blue jeaned, cowboy-hatted group. He'd dressed the part with a long sleeve denim shirt that covered his tattoos. The lead singer, a shapely red-haired woman wore an American Flag mini dress that echoed the one pinned to the pub's wall. Not the Blaspherian type.

Nell and I ordered the oyster burgers with bacon and a side of fries to share. I watched Jimmy do a riff on his saxophone. This group played country. He paid no attention to the audience in the room and hadn't seen me yet.

I leaned close to Nell and cupped my hand to make myself heard. "I feel like I'm stalking him."

"You are," she said matter-of-factly.

I knew I was going down a rabbit hole of questionable decisions, but once I'd started, I kept going. "He's hurting his daughter. He thinks he's protecting her by hiding her, but she'll keep getting sicker."

Jimmy finished his riff and saw me in the audience. He whispered to the singer and stepped off the stage in our direction. "My newest fans, eh?"

"You're good," I admitted and introduced him to Nell. "We're in the area on family business and I'm still looking for Laurel. I'm worried about her, Jimmy. She's not well enough to be out of treatment" I felt him pull away. "I think she's with you." I listed the signs—how he suddenly had keys to her apartment and seemed to be there to collect her belongings.

He shook his head. "You've gone rogue, Miss Grace. Tracking escaped patients across county lines is unusual, even for the mental health system."

There wasn't much else I could do unless Laurel showed up at the bar, but I tried making an earnest argument anyway. "Even though she said she killed her therapist," I reminded him.

"I don't believe it." Jimmy said. He smoothed his long beard, his hair, and his shirt, but he couldn't contain the emotion in his eyes.

"I don't either, but shouldn't we be sure?"

"Oh man, I can't help you. I've got to play."

The singer in the flag dress made eye contact from across the room and Jimmy waved. She motioned for him to hurry.

"How long will you be here?" I asked.

"All week. This place will get busier every day."

I looked up, surprised to see the Pub coming alive with people arriving and waiting for the music. The electric guitar player wailed a riff that vibrated the room, and all eyes went to the stage.

Jimmy turned to join the band and the Pub's door banged open in the silent space that followed. A white-haired man whose bushy beard and girth could have gotten him a job as Santa, grabbed at the door and struggled to pull it closed as if the wind had blown him in and fought back. Dried leaves scattered across the floor. He scanned the room, saw Jimmy James, and headed over.

"Jimmy!" he bellowed in a voice that carried over the music. "This ain't working. Gotta talk to you."

"Patrick, my man." Jimmy put his arm around the newcomer and shook his hand. The waitress appeared with a draft beer before being asked. Jimmy directed him toward the stage. "I've got a seat for you by the stage. We'll let these ladies enjoy their dinner."

The man's eyes twinkled as he focused on us ladies. "I could entertain them a while," He said with a flirtatious lilt to his voice, his cheeks were flushed from broken capillaries. He sucked the foam from the beer and smiled at Nell, "You're a pretty girl, do you play pool?"

Even in the dim lighting, I saw Nell color and straighten her shoulders. Her *No* was firm. Ill-advised attention from an older man wasn't going over well with her. Jimmy maneuvered himself between the stocky white-haired man and Nell. "Don't think I'm not worried," he said to me, then backed the man named Patrick away from our table. He looked stocky and strong in spite of the belly.

"Creep," Nell said.

I agreed. Nell and I finished our food without much gusto. I went up to the bar to pay and Nell went to get the car, angling to the door to avoid Santa's gaze. Jimmy James was on a saxophone solo which showed just how hard it was to make money in the music business even if you were *very* good. I didn't listen to much country music and thought sax might not fit, but the sultry sound took the song to a higher level. Jimmy leaned into the music and I felt his loneliness drift over the listening room and pull the crowd along with him. I was sure Laurel was with him and I thought that she was not going to cure his sadness.

Nell brought the Prius to the street in front of the pub. Her hands clenched the wheel in a stronger reaction than I'd expect. "Did Santa get to you?" I asked, climbing in.

She gave me a scornful look to let me know that wasn't the issue. "It is not Santa," she said. "I saw the man from the homeless count. Now he's following us."

Chapter 15

Nell pressed the gas, speeding away too fast for the small-town streets. There was no one in sight now.

"You saw Theo Martinez? I asked.

"He was on the terrace watching the door. I came out, and he stepped into the shadows. When I brought the car and I saw him in that old green SUV. It's a Honda. He cruised by very slowly like he was trying to intimidate me."

Caesar paced in the back of the Prius, sensing our anxiety. I turned to reassure him,   glad we brought him. I scanned the surroundings. The road to I-5 was dark and straight. This part of the state was known for growing tulips, berries, and seed crops. The flat, well-tended fields also gave good sightlines. There was no car now, but I'd never forgive myself if I'd put Nell in danger.

"He seems to be watching Laurel's family. Maybe it's not us," I said, still scanning behind as Nell turned onto the freeway. After a beat, another set of headlights came on the same entrance. "But maybe it is. There's someone, but it's impossible to tell what kind of car."

We drove north, retracing our trip to Mount Vernon. We wouldn't turn off until Burlington.

"Bad news about our Airbnb," Nell said. "It's a cabin in the woods on the road to Sedro Woolley. I thought it would be nice..."

"But now it's too isolated." I finished her sentence. "That car is still back there. Same distance."

"There must be motels in town." Nell watched the rear-view mirror.

I pulled out my phone to check. "Two. We can do a drive by and pick one." Paying the rent for two places was no problem for a little peace of mind.

"Are you getting too close to this murderer?"

"It sure doesn't feel like it. You know, I never heard back from Nate about this Theo Martinez, guy's arrest." He'd been at work and might have more information. I punched in his number, but no one answered their phone anymore. Nate's message came on and I asked for an update, telling him that the man was too close for comfort and we needed to know.

The road toward Sedro Woolley was dark and disfigured by logging. We were out of tulip country now. There were occasional cars in either direction. I couldn't tell if anyone was still following us. The wind that started back at the pub, gusted from the north, shaking the car. We passed the address for the cabin which was set down a long driveway in a stand of fir trees. As Nell slowed to check it out, a barn owl swooped in front of the car, so close that its heart-shaped white face stayed imprinted on my eyes after it dipped down to the roadside.

"Did you see that?" Nell asked and punched the gas again as if we were the prey.

At the edge of town, we passed a shabby looking motel on Route 20 and kept going to the Three Rivers Inn which looked more upscale but had an unsettling empty parking lot. Nell turned around and headed back to the one with more activity. I watched the side streets along the way in case Martinez had pulled off to watch, but it was too dark to do much good.

We walked Caesar around the well-lit parking lot and checked in. For fifty dollars, the Skagit Motel accepted pets and was about what I'd expect—twin beds, an undercounter refrigerator and a hot plate. Like the Extended Stay, I could hear a television on the other side of the thin wall. I liked knowing someone was there. Nell changed into pajamas and settled in one bed with one of Rose's diaries. I took the bed closest to the window and startled at the sound of every car that passed on Route 20. Just when I'd finally dropped into a restless sleep, Nell shook me awake and waved the diary. "Listen to this."

I threw off the covers and propped myself on an elbow. The room was over heated.

"Grandma Rose hadn't written for a while," Nell said. She sat up straight in the narrow bed. The frayed white tee shirt she always slept in was stretched at the neck and the asymmetrical haircut accentuated her jawline. "I figure that happened when she was depressed. Then in May, she writes *It's good Grace is going to Duvall for the summer.*"

My heart thudded. Mom's worries always became my worries. "Why?"

"She says *I'm afraid I'm going crazy too.*"

I reached over to touch the book, covered in a beautiful cloth binding in blue and green swirls with the year penned neatly on the front corner. "I turned ten that year, but I never saw her have symptoms—like I see at work. Did she say what felt crazy?"

"She'd talked to your dad. He'd heard something from friends and didn't think she could take care of you."

I snorted in disbelief. "There was no risk of him taking me. He was in a commune in Oregon."

"On the contrary, there were lots of kids in that commune and he had a new girlfriend who wanted kids too. You, for instance."

The idea of my father, who never bothered to visit, thinking he had any claim made me bristle. "Well that never happened. What else does it say?"

"Grandma Rose wondered if it might be better for you."

Nell and I looked at each other in silence, a heavy silence. I sat up on edge of the bed, reclining felt wrong. "Poor Mom," I said with all the mixed feelings I usually had when thinking about our shared past. "What then?"

"Then you went to Duvall for the summer like you always did."

The next morning, we didn't see the Honda SUV and headed to Sedro Woolley for coffee. An early morning fog blurred the roads and houses. The main street had a wide, straight run to accommodate the logging trucks and a view toward the Cascade Mountains dimly visible through the haze. It had the raw look of the Northwest towns that never added niceties like shade trees after cutting the surrounding forest, but the brick store fronts had been cleaned up in a recent economic revival. Logging, mining, and the state psychiatric hospital with its adjoining dairy farm had once been the area's economic engines. Now Sedro Woolley was scrambling to find its next new resource.

The Hometown Café, a big room lined with booths, seemed to be the place for breakfast, but toast and coffee were all I wanted. Nell slipped out of her coat, a retro, chestnut colored affair that flared at the knee. She'd dressed up for our visit to the old state hospital.

I checked messages while we waited.

She made eye contact and mouthed "Nate?"

I nodded when his voice came on. "It's Tuesday morning. The news about Theo Martinez isn't good. He was arrested on suspicion of murder in 1988. The victim was his brother. He was stabbed in a room above a bar outside of Bellingham. Martinez was released but the case never closed. I suggest you avoid him."

I passed the phone for Nell to listen.

"His brother was stabbed. Marion Warfield was killed with a knife." Nell said and followed with a guttural sound in her throat.

"Maybe he does think we are too close. Glad we didn't spend the night in the cabin."

We finished our second cup of coffee, both lost in our own thoughts—mine went from Theo Martinez to Annie, Laurel and finally to my grandmother. The waitress told us about her sister who had postpartum depression before giving us directions to the old Northern State campus. When we left, Main Street was quiet. There was no sign we were being followed.

On Fruitdale Road, we found a stately, but empty hospital gatehouse flanked by classic lampposts. A lane lined with black limbed trees that had already lost their leaves curved ahead, but a road sign warned us to turn back. The chatty waitress had told us the campus was designed by the Olmstead Brothers, from the family of famous landscape architects who designed Central Park in New York. The hospital had been emptied and closed in the seventies, twenty years after my grandmother died there. Following

Lily Van der Meer's directions, we found one of the remaining California Mission Style buildings which now housed a work training program.

Lily V, as she introduced herself, grasped first my hand, then Nell's in an energetic grip. She was tiny like her sister, but different in every other way. Her white pixie cut framed a wrinkled and well-scrubbed face. She trotted along in scuffed New Balance walking shoes and led us to the high-ceilinged office in back that stored the hospital's historical records.

"I'll make tea." She busied herself putting classic Lipton into white paper cups and motioned us to a pair of heavy chairs. I was drawn to the shelves of pale green books lining the wall. I ran my finger along their bindings, each labeled by year. Lily V came up behind me and took my hand, guiding it to the register marked 1949-1950. "Bring it over," she said.

I carried the book to the desk where we pulled our chairs so we could all see. Inside the book, page after page of old-fashioned handwriting listed names and admission dates, followed by more columns.

"How will I ever find her?" I asked.

"I looked her up when you called. They're numbered." Lily V pointed to the first column with numbers in the five hundreds. She handed me a piece of white paper folded lengthwise with 587 written on one corner. Then it was easy to find Lucy Mae Cooper.

I looked over at Nell. Her eyes were sad. Then I placed the folded paper under my grandmother's name as a marker. Nell came and rested her chin on my shoulder so we could read it together. The register listed all the information we'd found on the death certificate and finally, two columns headed Date of last Treatment and Date of Release.

"Her final treatment was 1/19/1950, my mother's 10th birthday, I said."

"Final treatment," Nell repeated and pointed to the line in the book. "Same as the date of her release, which was really the date of her death."

"I'm so sorry," Lily said and glanced from me to Nell. I'd told her

I worked with people with serious mental illness, so she directed her answer to Nell. "There weren't many options in those days— Electroconvulsive Therapy—they still use a more refined form ECT for serious depression, Insulin Coma Therapy, Lobotomy."

"A horror," Nell said. "I've been reading my grandmother's diaries. She was just a girl when her mother was sent up here to Northern State. Later, she learned her mom got the insulin coma therapy."

"That was horrible, but it was a horror without treatment too. They were still doing that when I started here, but I didn't work on those units." Lily V sat with her hands folded on her lap and regarded them for a moment. "Your mom knows what it's like when people are so sick. The nurses who did those treatments told me it was like a miracle when it helped. To see people get a little better."

Nell looked at the dates again. "She died just two weeks after her admission—of a heart attack."

"She would have gotten insulin injections until she went into a coma. Six days a week. That therapy was stopped in the '60s, of course. It was just too hard physically and medications were starting to come out."

Even though the date was more than fifty years ago, the loss seemed fresh because we were just learning about it. We sipped our tea quietly for a few minutes. I thought about Jimmy James losing his son to suicide. There were no easy answers with mental illness. It could be dangerous with treatment or without it. Lily V, with her small stature and white hair, stared at her folded hands. I thought she looked like a statue, maybe a saint for helping the people who may not get better. Finally, she spoke. "I've been tending the graves of people who died here. I talk to a lot of families, trying to reunite them with the patients who died here. What's different about today is," she took my hand again. "I knew your mother and your grandmother."

"What do you remember?" I asked, afraid to hear.

"I'd just started high school. I'd been your mother's babysitter for a long time. Mrs. Lucy, your grandmother, her husband never came back from World War II, so she was single. She seemed so much younger than the other moms, less matronly. She was fun. She was okay," Lily said with emphasis. "I never saw her have troubles in the years I was growing up."

"Oh," I said, thinking of the many families struggling with unanswered questions about mental illness I'd met over the years. Now I was one of them.

"Your sister, Iris, told us about the piano," Nell said.

"I remember that and the very next day, Rose ran to our house for help. She was terrified. I went with Rose. Mrs. Lucy was in the back yard, digging a hole in the pouring rain and talking to her voices. It was like a grave.

"Then she said, *Get in. Get in, Rosy. I have to hide you from the ghosts.* I moved in front of Rose to protect her. I knew she'd have buried the girl alive."

We sat, imagining the scene. Another memory I couldn't quite capture seemed close—like the day I'd heard the screen door slam on my way into the kitchen. It was the diary Nell was reading the night before. The book in its watery-looking binding and deckle paper was a gift I chose for Mom that Christmas. I was the same age as Mom was when Lucy died. I did go to my grandparents' house in Duvall when school let out. That summer was different.

"In the attic here," Lily's words brought me out of my thoughts, "there are shelves full of unclaimed belongings. We can see if there's anything of your grandmother's there."

Nell and I followed her single file out of the room and down the hall with sloping wood floors to a locked door. Lily pulled a key out of her pocket and led us up a set of stairs to a room in the eaves with light bulbs hanging from open rafters. Dusty moths circled and disappeared, a reminder of my mother's upstairs room. Open shelves with hard sided suitcases, wooden crates and foot lockers were labeled with numbered Manilla paper tags.

"We are looking for 587," Lily said.

A part of me hoped that we wouldn't find anything, that Lucy's family had come to lovingly retrieve her belongings in their time of loss. A much larger part hoped that that there would be something here for Nell and me after all these years. Nell touched my arm, the same anticipation I felt reflected in her face.

We followed the numbered shelves. There at shoulder level, we found 587. A tan suitcase with leather trim and a cardboard tag with Grandma Lucy's name. I stood, afraid to touch it.

Lily stepped back to let us get closer. "Go ahead. You can sign a form downstairs. It's yours."

Nell pulled the suitcase off the shelf and we followed Lily downstairs.

"The last thing I can offer you is her grave," Lily said. She gave us directions to the hospital cemetery and told us to look for 587 again. She said there would be no name.

The door leading out of the old hospital was flanked by oversized sash windows. On the way out, Nell's heels clicked on the old wooden floor, and she paused in the entryway with the suitcase. Her silhouette in the old-fashioned coat was backlit by the windows. For a moment, I imagined her as my grandmother Lucy, finally able to leave the mental institution. The fog had lifted, but another front seemed to be moving in. Dark clouds hung in the east, edged by sunlight. Long shadows marked the grounds.

Chapter 16

Back at the car, I clipped on Caesar's leash to let him out. Nell balanced the old-fashioned suitcase on the edge of the open hatch and tried to slide the brass buttons to release the clasps, but nothing moved. "I can't believe it's locked."

Caesar tugged on the lead in the opposite direction—he wanted a walk. I wanted nothing more than to break the locks to get inside, but I felt Nell's hand on my arm.

"At home," she said. "Maybe we'll find something in that box of keys."

"Maybe." I gave up on the suitcase. My head felt like it was wrapped in cotton wool and my ears buzzed. I hadn't begun to process what I'd heard about my grandmother trying to bury my mother alive.

"I'll drive," Nell whispered. When we got to the empty guard house, she braked and pointed in the direction of the graveyard. The green SUV waited on the berm 100 yards down the road. I could read its license plate from where I sat.

"I knew it," she said softly as if he could overhear. "We didn't see him, but he's there."

Nell hesitated between the ivy-covered lamp posts, then made a turn away from the car—and the graveyard we'd meant to visit. She drove toward town.

I pictured Theo Martinez smoking cigarettes on the highway all night. He never bothered us. "Where are we going?"

"Back to the café," Nell said. "Pretty sure he'll come along. But we need a plan."

That woke me up.

Nell adjusted the rearview mirror and watched while she drove. "He's keeping his distance, but still there."

In town, an empty parking place opened right in front of the Hometown Café where we'd bought our morning coffee. We chose a table this time and scanned the menu. Breakfast was served all day and we both ordered pancakes and bacon, now the go-to meal to acknowledge family loss. The sweet and salt on my tongue made everything seem okay, or at least the best it could be, at the moment. I ate slowly and felt Nell's eyes on me.

"I'm glad you thought of this," I said.

Nell smiled and slid out of her seat and checked the front window. When she came back, she reported. "He's at the end of the block."

"I'm almost ready to have a talk with Mr. Martinez." I was getting fed up.

"You're kidding," Nell said.

"He could follow us all the way back home and I don't want that. If I talk to him out there—at least it's a public place, and daytime.

I didn't like the idea of walking right up to him while he watched. I wanted more control. Or surprise. I paid for breakfast and asked the waitress if there was a back exit we could use, but before she led through the kitchen to the alley, Nell paused. "I'm going to get Caesar. Watch for me and we'll meet at his car at the same time."

In spite of Nell's exposure, I knew the dog could be protective. We split up. I put my phone in my pocket, ready to dial 911 if needed. Out in the alley, the exhaust fan blew air laden with hot grease. I passed dumpsters and broken-down boxes and came out into brightness—the sun had found a slot between clouds. From the corner, the SUV was a few cars down, angled into a space. Theo Martinez sat with his elbow on the frame of the car's open window wearing a down coat. He watched Nell and Caesar walking up the street. A pair of women browsed the window of the fabric store, I hoped the sidewalk was busy enough for safety. I nodded to Nell, and we converged at the car.

"Mr. Martinez," I said.

He clambered out of the car, slamming the door behind him.

I fought the impulse to step back. Nell came shoulder to shoulder with me, holding Caesar on a short leash—he strained toward the man.

"How do you know my name?"

"The Seattle police. I copied your license number when we saw you in Duvall. I wondered then why you were watching the Elegant Beast. Now I wonder why you are watching me." I kept my tone calm and serious.

Martinez took the step back.

Nell spoke next, confident. "You've been following us since yesterday. We're two women traveling. You're scaring us."

I caught Nell's eye in a nonverbal signal of support. She had good instincts with people, the same ones Annie once had, still had.

Today, Martinez was clean shaven, showing deep lines carved in his cheeks. It was the first time I'd seen him in the light. I thought he'd been spending his nights in the car, but his clothes looked new and unrumpled. He adjusted his glasses and squinted with the sun in his face. It seemed as if all the traffic and people had disappeared, and a spotlight was on him.

Caesar pulled toward the man. Then he leaned into Martinez' leg, wagging his tail and angling to be petted. Martinez offered his hand for him to smell. I thought the dog was a good judge of character, but there were things Caesar might not know.

"The police also told me you were arrested in the murder of your brother."

"I was released." Martinez coughed; his voice was rough from smoking.

"Released because there wasn't enough evidence," I countered because his release did not comfort me.

"No." He shook his head and coughed again. "That's why I'm here. I've been looking for my brother's murderer ever since. This is the closest I've come."

"Close? What have Nell and I got to do with that?"

"I think we're looking for the same thing." He leaned down and rubbed Caesar's neck. The dog looked up at him in bliss. I decided to hear him out.

"Well, come into the café then and tell us what you're looking for," I said. He would definitely be safer inside than following us around the countryside. Nell and I couldn't eat another bite, but I offered to buy him a meal. Inside, we settled back at the table and asked for tea. The waitress didn't seem surprised to see us for the third time in a day. Theo ordered the club sandwich.

"You spent all night watching our motel." I said accusingly.

He shook his head. "No, I wasn't there all night, but I sure didn't sleep enough. I wanted to be back in time to see where you were going."

"What does Northern State have to do with your brother's murder?"

"The hospital? Nothing. But you're watching Mo James and her daughter. So am I."

That stopped me. "I'm a mental health evaluator. Do you know where her daughter is?"

"Not yet." He took three huge bites of the sandwich and devoured a dill pickle before he spoke. "Sorry. I've just been eating junk food in the car. I'm starving."

I watched him eat, figuring the story had already waited. I got no scary vibes from him now. He just looked hungry.

Finally, Nell asked the important question. "What does this have to do with your brother?"

He took a deep breath and wiped his mouth with the paper napkin. The café receded when he began his story. "We grew up in Wenatchee. Our parents picked fruit, but we were going to be better. My brother worked thinning trees, and I worked all the time to save money to help him. Angel was only seventeen—he'd just been accepted to the UW, so I took him out to celebrate. I got him a fake ID and we went to a roadhouse."

The sandwich sat untouched now. "Angel started flirting with a girl—cute, blonde, intense. So, I left him to it and went out for a toke. The girl was there with her father, and last I saw, Angel was playing pool with the dad and girl was hanging on him. You know how they do." He sat back and pulled off his glasses. Without them he seemed more vulnerable.

"When I went back, they were all gone. The place had a few rooms to rent upstairs, and the bartender told me that Angel and the girl had gotten a room. I was pissed, and the bartender knew it. Here I was working all I could to save money for his education and he threw it away on a one-night stand. The bartender told me he was drunk. Angel and the father had been betting and Angel won every game. The dad bought him beer and whiskey every time. Angel was only seventeen. He couldn't handle it. I ran upstairs with no idea what I'd do, probably punch him out. I got there, and the room was open. Angel was down."

Theo closed his eyes before he went on. "Angel was collapsed on his back with his throat slit. He'd bled out. She did it with his own buck knife. I can still see the room—knotty pine walls—and hear the pool balls striking from downstairs." He folded his glasses and then reopened them getting finger smudges on the lenses.

"That must have been terrible," I said, and Nell agreed. We sat in silence for a moment. "Are you sure it was the girl who did it? Could it have been the father?" I asked.

He shook his head. "She did it. Then the girl was gone. The father was gone. All I remember was howling and I guess they found me with the knife in my hand kneeling beside him. That's how I got arrested. They let me go because there were other fingerprints on the knife—smaller, a girl's. It cleared me, but they never found a match for those and they never found her.

At the end of the story, I tried to piece together the meaning. A girl. A slit throat like Laurel's therapist. "What makes you think it was Mo James?"

"I spent years looking. Turns out that a father and daughter had been in small towns all over Washington. They were a regular con team. Her flirting, him losing at pool to get their marks drunk. Then she'd rob them, wallets, watches, whatever. People in bars told me about it. Local newspapers reported it. But there was never another after the murder. Angel was the only one."

"Why Mo James?" I asked again. "She doesn't look like a con artist." But I thought to myself, it might explain why she was a runaway as a girl.

"I stopped looking a long time ago." Theo said. "It wasn't going to bring my brother back and nobody ever made it to college. I moved over here to the Skagit Valley and supervised farm workers who came up from Oaxaca. It's good enough work. Then, the other day I was in that bar in Conway. I saw her." His face showed the surprise he must have felt.

"Her?" I asked.

"The same girl. Young. Blonde hair, intense brown eyes. A little heavier, but she even moved the same. I thought I saw a ghost. The bartender said she'd been asking questions—she had family up here and wanted to learn about them. Then the guy showed me the Seattle Sunday paper. An article about a new restaurant. The Elevated Beast. There was a picture of the woman who owned it and her daughter who was the spitting image of the girl who killed Angel." He laughed bitterly. "I finally found her when I stopped looking."

I believed he might be right, but it didn't seem enough to prove that Mo was his brother's killer. I shook my head, not quite able to make the connections.

"I've got notebooks full of information about the con." He pulled out his wallet, extracted a yellowed clipping and slid it across the table. The article described the father and daughter and the same scam. "This sums it up."

"How can you be sure?"

"I wasn't," he said. "Until the old man came in. He had the same bushy beard twenty years ago. Now it's white. I'd recognize him anywhere. He stayed with the girl, Laurel, all evening. He taught her to play pool."

Nell and I looked at each other. The man with the Santa Claus beard had asked Nell to play pool too.

"He was there last night," Nell said.

Theo nodded, "I saw."

Nell studied the heavy ceramic cup in front of her. "So, now that you've found them. What are you going to do?"

Chapter 17

Theo Martinez looked tired. All the lines on his face were pulled down with the weight of sadness. Voices in conversation and the clattering of plates and flatware were the background to our conversation. The smell of vinegar rose from the puddle left by the dill spear on Theo's plate. Bitter.

"It's a good thing I didn't find her back then. I probably would have killed her, just because I was young and angry." He looked me in the eye while he answered Nell's question. "I have no idea what I want now. I just keep watching. There's no work in the fields now so I have all the time in the world.

"I think you wasted your time following us," Nell said "If you wanted to find Laurel, you should have stuck with the grandfather. That's probably where she is."

Nell's words rang true which made me wonder if Theo really wanted to find Laurel at all. I watched him take his glasses off and polish them on a faded bandana. After all this time, I thought what he really wanted was an ally.

He finally spoke. "What I want is some kind of justice. The girl needs to know about her family. I'll tell her they killed my brother." He said it with a mix of weariness and determination.

I felt protective of them all: Laurel, Mo, Theo. I imagined Mo's life twenty years ago. Traveling around the countryside with her red-faced father, flirting, and conning men. How old could she have been? Not old enough to be in a bar, but neither was Theo's brother. I thought about how Mo, now successful, had recreated herself. I thought about murder—not one but two. It was impossible to think through the implications.

"Laurel should know about her family," I said. "But when and how are delicate questions. She's very ill."

"No kidding," Theo said.

"Normally, when her psychosis stabilized, she would work it through with her therapist." Even as I said it, I wondered if Laurel knew already, but I wasn't about to discuss the dead therapist with him.

Nell, however, was. She cradled her teacup and spoke in a low voice. "But her therapist was murdered. Did you know that?"

Theo sat up straight, alert now. He shook his head no.

"We thought you were the killer," Nell continued.

"When was she killed?"

I told him the timeline. "But the thing is how. Her therapist's throat was slit."

"Twenty years later," Theo said. "I was starting to have some sympathy for the woman. Now I think the girl was looking for the truth about the family and her mother stopped it, with a knife again."

Theo drew into himself, but I sensed his old anger kindling, an anger that had driven him for many years. I hoped this wouldn't renew his search for justice, whatever justice would look like to him at this point.

Nell and I exchanged looks and I shook my head slightly to communicate that we would not be telling Theo that, true or not, Laurel had said she was the killer. Had she followed in her mother's footsteps? It was too much. All I knew for sure was that there was a danger. But I didn't know if Laurel was in danger or if she was the danger. Either could explain why she wanted to escape.

"I've got to find Laurel," I said to Theo. "If you find her first, please stay calm. You've been waiting a long time. You aren't in a hurry. Call me." I dug in my purse for a piece of paper. I wrote my phone number down and slid it across the table with the pen.

Theo wrote his, ripped the paper in half and slid it back to me.

After he left, Nell looked disturbed. "Do you think he can let it go?"

"He's not our biggest worry. I hope." Though I didn't know what was. I pulled out my phone to check my messages—no word from Annie.

A passing rain cloud spilled over town. Nell and I ran to the car and slammed the doors. Caesar paced in the back; he'd been cooped up far too long. We had time before we needed to head home. "We have to visit the graves," I said.

"You don't sound like you want to," Nell said.

"It's a responsibility. No more family secrets left to fester. Look at Laurel's story." The sins of the fathers—or the mothers—never failed to be visited upon the children, I thought.

Caesar's breath had steamed the windows and I grabbed a rag from the glove box.

"We should run Caesar first," Nell said. "But we don't want him disturbing the dead at the cemetery."

Nell twisted in her seat to pull off her good coat and trade it for the chartreuse puffer with a raincoat to put over it. She'd brought a lot of coats.

"We'll take him to the dairy farm where the patients used to work. It's a park now." I pulled onto the highway, no longer worried about being followed. The old farm was only minutes away. We left the car near a picnic shelter and set off uphill toward the first building, a long barn with a rusty corrugated roof. Caesar cut frantic circles, chasing birds into grassy mounds. Fields ran beyond and the North Cascades rose, higher and closer than where we lived. Rain clouds moved in and out of the rocky peaks. Nell and I walked past a collapsed outbuilding, nothing but a roof on the ground.

In its day, the setting was better for a person with mental illness. I looked around at the pastures and outbuildings and imagined the patients would have grown food and tended animals instead of watching tv. The mental health system sometimes failed—then and now. My grandmother's treatment didn't help, it killed her. Today's system was designed for community placements, but when funding was cut, it turned out to be jail or tents by the freeway. The next cloudburst rolled over the fields, just ahead. I looked for the rainbow but couldn't find one.

When the rain reached us, Nell and I ducked under a metal roof that was still standing. I stepped over a curb and realized we were entering what must have been the slaughterhouse. A cement floor sloped to a drain and a yellow metal panel that seemed designed to funnel the animals to their fate had rusted and streaked from the wet. Graffiti had been spray-painted across the panel; it read *YOU ARE AMONG THE FORGOTTEN*.

Nell moved closer and traced the letters with a finger, then turned the words around. "The forgotten are here," she said. "Your grandmother. It runs in families. It could be you or me someday."

I agreed. "Either of us."

Nell didn't move. "The forgotten," She said and rubbed her hands to warm them. "We never looked in the bag you brought from the motel."

Forgotten. I whistled for Caesar and we headed for the car.

At the car, I lifted the hatch and reached for the black plastic bag. Then I found a couple pairs of nitrile gloves in my purse, glad I'd taken them from the cleaning cart at Extended Stay. Nell carried the bag to the shelter, holding it at arms-length.

"I can't believe we didn't check this before." Nell said.

She knelt on the cold concrete by the garbage can and pulled out a layer of rotten food. Finally, we reached crumpled papers. I smoothed notebook pages on the damp cement floor of the picnic shelter and sorted envelopes from paper.

"Someone still writes letters by hand," I said. "They're addressed to Laurel not Jimmy."

I picked up the envelopes and noticed the writing was so firm it ripped the paper. The return address was in Conway, Washington. "These are from her grandfather," I said.

Nell glanced and added more to the stack. "Let's see."

I chose a sheet of lined paper and started to read. The words were rambling and disorganized, but the themes were easy to pick up—he wanted to see her. *You come up here and I'll take care of you. I'm not too busy I have chickens and goats for you to play with but you're not a little girl. I miss you even though we've never met.*

I have stories to tell you about when your mother was a girl too. It went on for pages and was signed *Your Loving Grandfather.*

I stopped reading, rocked back, and sat on my heels. "What stories do you think he tells?"

Nell had finished sorting and shook the pile of letters to remove and final crumbs. "Probably about playing pool. Here's the return address."

Nell plugged the address into her phone.

"The graves," I said. "Maybe…"

"We have time for both."

"I need to think," I said. "When we scattered Mom's ashes, I felt so unprepared. I want to say something for Grandma Lucy when we get there."

Nell wrapped the letters back into a plastic bag and made a pile of the rest of the garbage. She snapped off the gloves and tossed them in too. "Annie would know what to say."

"Annie," I echoed. That brought back a different worry. The cold from the ground seeped through my feet and I felt frozen.

My phone rang in my hip pocket and I pulled it out. Annie's name and photograph filled the screen as if we'd summoned her.

Chapter 18

Annie's name on my phone brought a flood of relief mixed with anger. Where was she and how could she have put me through this worry? I took the call, determined to stay in control and not to let my irritation show.

"God damn it, Annie. Where are you?" I'd failed the control test.

"Shaw Island," she said.

"In the San Juans?" I put the phone on speaker so Nell could hear too. Shaw Island was home to several orders of nuns. Annie had stayed there before, with the Benedictines who raised heirloom sheep and cows at their isolated monastery.

"I'm sorry, Grace. I needed to reflect. I was going to contact you when I got here, but cell phones are sketchy and the windstorm took out the landline, electricity, internet. Everything."

The windstorm on the night of the All-Home Count seemed so long ago.

"Anyway," she said, "I'm on retreat at Our Lady of the Rock. I learned to use a chainsaw and cleared two downed trees to get up the hill where I'd have reception." She sounded young and happy.

"You could have told me before you left town. I've been calling everywhere. Going crazy." I said, almost ready to give up my churlishness. I knew she needed time to heal.

"I know. You have a lot on your mind," she said through crackles on the line. "Especially with Laurel and your mom. Are you at home?"

"No. Nell and I are in Sedro Woolley. At the old Northern State Hospital."

"You're on retreat too."

"Not exactly. Maybe. I have a lot to tell you." I stood and brushed debris from the knees of my jeans.

"I bet," her voice had a strange sadness. "You're close. Come to the island. It's only half an hour to the Anacortes Ferry from where you are."

I looked in the direction of the graveyard, shrouded by clouds moving in from the mountains, then toward the road leading to Annie.

"Please come," she said. "I need to see you. We'll talk—I promise."

I was touched that Annie felt a need to see me too. Nell hadn't chimed in, but now she was nodding, and mouthing *let's go*. She was already on her phone checking the ferry schedule. I agreed to visit the island. After all my worry about Annie, I thought she was doing better than I was.

"Okay," I said. "But first we have to stop in Conway. I think Laurel may be there with her Grandfather."

"May be…" Annie began, then cut herself off. "Just come," she said and gave directions from the island ferry terminal.

After I said good-bye, I looked toward the graveyard again. Today, my main concern had to be the living. I finally knew Annie was okay, I wanted to find Laurel next.

Nell touched my arm. "We'll come back to the grave another day. Grandma Lucy has been waiting a long time."

I smiled. "By then, I'll know what to say."

We stuffed the rest of the debris from Jimmy's room into the garbage can. I glanced back at the old dairy before we left. The dark clouds moved southwest, the same as we would, but so far, the next rain held off.

On the way out of Sedro Wooley, the landscape changed from logging country pressed against the mountains, to the ordered fields of the valley. We passed farm stands with piles of knobby pumpkins and signs saying Cider for sale.

"We're close to the place we watch the snow geese," Nell said. "As a matter of fact, we are here." The area was a winter pilgrimage for birdwatchers when thousands of migrating geese filled the sky before settling into wet fields. Farmers planted winter wheat to encourage them.

"Arrive at destination," Siri's computerized voice reported from the dashboard, affirming what Nell said. We had reached the address we found in Laurels' grandfather's letter. The greening fields were pocked with standing water from the recent storm. No geese today. The address was across from the rutted parking area where we'd watched geese the year before. We'd noticed the house then, dingy white and poorly kept. My shoulders tensed.

"What do we do if Laurel is there?" Nell asked. "Her father hates treatment, her grandfather is a con man, and her mother is a murderer."

"The family is a problem," I said in understatement and looked at Nell, wondering if I should involve her in this. I sat looking at the empty field wishing for a visitation of snow geese, but they hadn't yet arrived from their northern breeding grounds. "At least her mother won't be here," I said. "If Laurel is, she needs to get out and go back to the hospital."

"You'll never get her to do that," Nell said.

"There's a bench warrant. I'd have to call the police. I think she'll go back to Harborview unless they've found enough evidence to charge her. Then it would be jail." I remembered a former army colonel who had told his wife he'd shot and killed a friend and left the body in the trunk of his car. We evaluated the colonel for suicidal ideation, though he never admitted to a murder. Psych units don't accept felons, but they had to admit him until the police found the body to prove there had been a crime.

"This could be messy, Nell. Are you sure you want to be involved in this? The father or grandfather might be more a problem than Laurel." As I said it, I thought about how confidently she had handled our confrontation with Theo.

She raised one eyebrow with skepticism, an expression she'd inherited from me. "Safer with the two of us."

"I hope." I had visions of angry family members and the Shaw Island ferry drifting away without us. "If we do find Laurel, we can try to talk her into going back to the hospital, then leave when she says no. We wouldn't call the police while we're in the house."

Nell put her hand on the car door handle but didn't open it. "If she's there, let's take her out to eat. Feed the Hungry is today's plan."

"Whether or not Laurel is hungry."

"Theo sure was."

I tried to imagine Jimmy, or the grandfather agreeing to this dinner date and hoped they wouldn't be there.

"We'll see," I said.

We walked across the road to the house, A worn travel trailer was parked in front on the bare yard and two hens flapped in the small dry patches in the earth underneath. On our way to the front porch, Nell stepped around a desiccated squirrel, hind quarters eaten to the bone before being abandoned by its predator. We made eye contact and at the same moment, took deep breaths to steel ourselves, then walked up the steps. The covered porch was full of weathered boards, piles of damp clothing and two overflowing garbage cans. The smell of rotting food was here too.

Nell knocked and the door swung open as if Laurel had been waiting. She stood barefoot in the entry, in the same white shirt she'd been wearing in the hospital, stained, and crumpled after all these days.

"Oh," she said, pushing her now oily bangs from her forehead where a swath of pimples had broken out since I'd last seen her. Her face was puffy and pale. "The mental health evaluator. I forget your name."

"Grace Vaccaro," I reminded.

She stepped forward and leaned into my shoulder like a small child who needs to be hugged. I held her lightly. Her shoulders shook with sobs.

"What's wrong?"

She shook her head, still pressed into my shoulder.

Too broad a question, I realized. "Is your grandfather here?" I asked out of concern for how this visit might proceed if he was.

"No," she said taking a step back and wiping her face with her dirty shirt sleeve.

"Your father?"

"He wouldn't stay here. He's with some new girlfriend."

I looked around the front room. I wouldn't have stayed either. The house was cold and as disordered as Laurel's apartment, but here the disorder had been accumulating much longer. Boxes covered in dust and plates of dried food competed for space. The only way to get in was to follow narrow paths through broken furniture awaiting repair.

Nell stepped forward and introduced herself. "I'm Grace's daughter. You look hungry. Have you eaten today?"

Laurel shook her head. "There's no food."

"We could get something to eat." Nell pushed her plan.

Laurel said yes but looked around. "I know it sounds bad, but I can't find my shoes."

Before Nell helped her look, I asked Laurel if she would agree to go to a hospital. Her answer was a firm no.

I thought about the bare feet, the unheated house and lack of food that showed Laurel really couldn't care for herself. The professional in me wanted to call the police to get her back to treatment. The mother in me wanted to feed her.

Nell and Laurel came out, still without shoes. "No luck," Nell said. "I'll get my slippers."

"Do you have your medicine?" I asked Laurel while Nell ran to the car.

"Jimmy—my father—threw it away."

"Do you want it?" I said, cringing at the thought of searching the garbage.

"Yes. I was taking it every day until he found out. The demons are back." Laurel hugged her bare arms to warm herself.

I considered the options. We could leave and call the police like I'd planned. Or Nell and I could wait with Laurel for the police which, being nonemergent, could take a while. Any time, Jimmy or Patrick might return and sabotage it all.

I considered taking her to Shaw Island for the night, a very bad idea. I evaluated the risks. Was Laurel a murderer? In every interaction I'd had with her, in every level of her psychosis, she had never shown aggression. It was her mother with a history of violence. Still a bad idea.

Nell came back with a pair of shearling slippers and Frank's old shirt that she wore as a bathrobe. It was the only thing that would fit Laurel.

I thought about Laurel's medications and eyed the garbage, regretting that we'd used the last of the nitrile gloves. I opened the first black plastic can and couldn't believe my luck, right on top lay an amber bottle of medication, safely closed and intact with Laurel's name on it. I handed the pills to Laurel and we picked our way across the littered yard to the car. Nell let Caesar out to run. His boisterous energy caused Laurel to pull back.

"Don't worry," Nell said. "You sit up front with Mom."

Nell slid into the back seat and held the dog who tried to climb in with Laurel. I started the car and cranked up the heat.

Laurel was quiet, not showing the insightful façade I'd seen on the psychiatric unit. I found a granola bar and a bottle of water in my bag and offered them to her. She still held the pill bottle in both hands and seemed unable to let it go to take anything else.

"Is it time for those?" I asked, tilting my head toward the meds.

"It's twice a day," she answered. "I could start now and get back to my regular times in the morning."

Laurel slowly took out an oval blue pill. I capped the bottle for her and put it on the console, so she'd have free hands, then twisted the cap off the water bottle. After she swallowed the pill, I offered the granola bar, but she shook her head.

"Maybe real food will taste better," I told her. Just before I pulled onto the two-lane highway, we heard the eerie honking of snow geese. I put the window down and we listened and watched as a flock of thousands circled, white across the darkening sky, but didn't settle on the field. I felt sad when they moved on in search of something better.

I wanted to find a restaurant as far from Laurel's father and grandfather as possible and didn't stop until La Conner, an arty town on the Swinomish Channel. Visitors on daytrips wandered the old-fashioned main street with expensive shops selling everything from women's clothing to hand painted Italian dishes. I chose a nice view restaurant, thinking surely Patrick would not eat here and hoping Jimmy was more interested in late night activities. The lunch crowd was gone. Nell and Laurel stopped in the bathroom to clean up while the waitress led me to the table with the best view.

Laurel still walked woodenly when Nell escorted her back from the bathroom but looked a little more presentable. I thought about parents, like Jimmy, so distressed by the signs of illness that they blamed the symptoms on medications. Medications had dangers, but so did untreated mental disorders. The balance was hard to find.

Laurel sat and stared at the menu without seeming to take it in.

Nell was still in caregiver role. "They serve breakfast all day," she said. "Do you eat meat?"

Laurel nodded.

"How about pancakes and bacon?" Nell asked.

I couldn't help laughing.

"Okay." Laurel looked at me, perplexed, and smiled.

"Nell has a thing about pancakes,"

I remembered that Laurel had been so pleased to be getting to know her father and according to Theo, had been asking more questions about her family at the pub. For better or worse, she had her grandfather now too.

"How are things going? With getting to know your father and grandfather?"

She didn't respond.

"You told me about your father and how he supports you with 12 steps. What's your grandfather like?"

"He's too…" she drifted off and didn't answer for what seemed like a minute, "Much. Too much. They both threw away the medicine."

"You've always taken your medication," I repeated her earlier words.

"I did."

The pancakes came for Laurel and the salads Nell and I ordered to counterbalance our high sandwich intake on the road. We ate in silence watching a fishing boat with pale green gunwales unload across the channel. Laurel held her fork gingerly. The cuts on the inside of her hand had healed, but the puckered skin looked red and tender. She did go for the bacon and slowly wiped it through the syrup after each bite of pancake.

"How is your grandfather too much?"

"He tells stories. That's okay, but in them, he's always the best. The best carpenter, the best hunter, the best at raising livestock, fixing things, the best designer. He tells stories about my mom. In them, she's the best too. The best at butchering the livestock, the best cook." She looked at her last strip of bacon. "Well, that is true. But look at his house, the only thing he's best at is dreams."

Laurel seemed to be responding to the TLC, the medications couldn't be taking effect so soon. Color was coming back to her face and her movements seemed a little more spontaneous. I sat back and watched her eat, trying to process what I was learning. Mo had killed the young man in a bar. As a girl, she and her father ran cons in bars. Their usual ploy had probably gotten out of hand. A young man who couldn't handle liquor, a knife. What was his knife doing out?

Laurel quietly hummed while she was eating, the same song I'd heard when I evaluated her. A Tisket, A Tasket. No words this time. "I've been afraid to sleep," she said.

"How come?"

"I was always mad at my mother for keeping her family secret, but maybe she…I'm not sure. My grandfather makes me nervous. He taught me to play pool and seems to want me to—I don't know—take over my mom's place as his kid. He wants us to take a road trip."

Nell raised a brow and looked over at me. Already he was reimagining the con. I didn't think Laurel had discovered the killing, but Mo had to be worried she might. Worried that Laurel's contact with her own father, Patrick, would be anything but healthy.

I wasn't sure how Laurel's statements about killing her therapist fit, but I hoped her belief was metaphorical. Mo was the one with knife skills. It was Laurel's search that had led to Marion Warfield's murder.

I looked at my watch: 5:30. I had my own concern—Annie. I knew she was okay on the island, but I was thinking about the formal letter on my dining room table for the deposition. Did she have one too? She could lose the job she needed to finance the new degree. She was missing classes now. Annie needed to come home.

"What do you want to do now, Laurel?" I still wanted her to go to the hospital, but I didn't want to scare her away by insisting she go. I also didn't want to deal with it today.

She froze in response to my question, finally responding, "Where are you going?"

I shook my head. Everything I'd done since detaining Laurel had been an example of bad boundaries.

Nell answered before I could collect my thoughts. "We are going to Shaw Island. Annie is there. You know Annie."

Laurel's face relaxed into a smile. "Annie. I trust her."

Annie did have a magic about her. The idea seemed good in a worst-boundary kind of way. This situation wasn't normal, boundaries would have to stretch for now.

I sighed so deeply that both young women looked at me. "Okay. Annie's on retreat at a convent," I told Laurel. "Are you okay with a convent?"

She shrugged and said, "I've never been to one. Are you asking me to come?"

"Sure. I've got to call my husband Frank in case we lose phone service on the island."

Nell and Laurel nodded, already involved in looking up Our Lady of the Rock and talking about what to expect. I loved Nell's instincts for how to be around people with mental illness. She acted normal and engaged Laurel like anyone else.

While we waited for the ferry in Anacortes, I called Frank. The holding area was huge, maybe a dozen lanes destined for the islands. This evening they were nearly empty. The line of cars started to move while I told Frank about our day and our plan to visit Annie. Once our car boarded, Nell and Laurel went up to the sitting area and I stayed to talk privately. When I hung up, I had a voice mail from Nate, "The detectives on the murder case say they got Laurel James' belongings from the hospital. They were able to run DNA from the girl's bloody shirt. I thought the blood was from her wrists." He cleared his throat. "But only some of that belonged to Laurel, most of it was the therapists."

By the time I heard the message, the ferry had left the dock.

Chapter 19

The thrum from a ferry's engine usually made me sleepy, but not today. Laurel's head nodded on her chest, though. I studied her: the dirty blond hair, dark eyebrows, and blemished face. She smelled sour. Without medications, she lacked self-care. Her belly rolled over the top of her jeans and her forearms looked like a baby's, creased at the wrist from medication weight gain, but striped with cuts. Still, her intelligence and education showed. She did not look like a murderer, but neither did her mother. I thought Laurel was innocent and protecting her parent. That didn't explain the blood though.

Nell shared a seat with Laurel and gazed quietly out the window into the near darkness.

The San Juan Islands are made up of 172 islands and reefs dotting the waters between the United States and Canada. Shaw was the smallest island reachable by ferry. The islands looked like dark humps on the glassy water, covered in evergreens that absorbed what little light was left. The sky at the horizon held one last streak of red

Ours was the only car that disembarked at Shaw. The dock here, once famous for being staffed by nuns in full habit, was operated by the usual state workers—the nuns had aged and retired. The worker waved us onto the narrow two-lane road. My headlights showed fields and second growth forest with a comfortable island feel, as if everything here were scaled a little smaller than at home. I followed Annie's directions to Our Lady of the Rock; no sign announced it, only a rusty-armed cross hanging from a log frame. At the front of the property, a shake-shingled house was lit by a single bulb on the porch. Outbuildings and fenced pastures backed it and long-horned cows lowed, ambling over to inspect us. Nell put Caesar on a leash, and he trembled with interest at the beasts.

The house was empty. No one answered my knock. Then I saw a flashlight on the gravel road out of the trees. Annie walked down the hill to the house and her corn silk hair glowed without light. When she stepped on to the porch, she looked better than she had all year.

"Grace!" she wrapped me in a hug. "You made it."

"The place was deserted. I was losing hope," I joked.

"I saw you drive up all of two minutes ago."

"Listen to you, I thought a monastery retreat would make you more holy, not more sarcastic." It felt good to banter.

"I was at Vespers." She smiled beatifically, then she noticed Nell and Laurel unloading our duffels. "Laurel came." she whispered.

"It's a very long story," I answered.

Annie shook her head as if she didn't want to hear it and went to welcome them. She took the bags and led us up the worn wooden steps and into the unlocked house.

The living and dining rooms were simply furnished in comfortable old furniture that looked like it had been here since the seventies and wasn't new then. Books on saints and the contemplative life lined one wall. A table held a painted box with a sign asking for donations to help pay the costs for our lodging. I reached in my purse and fished out a handful of bills to cover the three of us.

In the dining room, a long table was set with mismatched plates and bowls. The scent of baking bread and something meaty came from the kitchen.

"Here," Annie led us to a hallway where each bedroom held a pair of single beds. "I'm putting Grace with me. We have some talking to do. Which bag?" Then she noticed only two bags for three people. "Did you bring anything?" she asked Laurel who shook her head no.

Annie showed Nell and Laurel their room and waved us toward the table, quickly adding another place setting. "The guest house is usually full. People come on retreat and work with the nuns. But it's late in the year—I'd have been alone tonight. I made beef stew and homemade bread to celebrate you coming."

Annie set a chipped enamel pot at her place at the table and bowed her head in prayer, blessing the food, those who eat it, the community, the world, and the spirit. She was very good at this chaplain business. We passed our bowls. Annie ladled while Nell cut thick slices of bread.

"The beef," I wondered aloud, "is it from the friendly cattle in the pasture?"

"Of course. On an island, everything comes by boat and stays forever, so self-sufficiency is best." Annie said.

Laurel spoke up. "I've helped my mom butcher meat for the restaurant. You're not squeamish if you grown up…" She ran out of words and began rocking and humming.

"Are you okay?" I put my hand on her arm to calm her. Nate's report about the therapist's blood on her clothing worried me. Even though I didn't want to think she was the murderer, I had to accept that it was still possible. Later, I'd secure the kitchen knives just in case. Laurel hadn't shown any threatening behavior, but she was stressed.

Laurel quietly nodded.

"The stew smells good," Nell said to Laurel, her focus still on eating. "Let's try it."

Laurel raised her spoon to her lips and tasted. Her shoulders relaxed. "It's good."

Nell and I added our agreement. The friendly cattle were delicious.

Annie gave an assessing look at Laurel and continued the calming distraction by talking about island routine while we ate. "*Ora et Labora* is what we do. Pray and work. She explained the hours of prayer that the nuns referred to as the Divine Office. She even attended matins in the middle of the night. "Mass is at 9:00 a.m. Then we have breakfast and work until the next prayer. I hope you'll participate." She looked at me when she said it.

I was skeptical but curious about the religious life and said yes to Mass and helping with the work. "We'll probably have to leave after *labora* though."

"Does a priest live here?" Nell asked.

"He comes every day—by ferry of course."

We talked more about the island, and after dinner Annie served a tea infused with lavender and lemon balm, all grown in the nuns' garden.

"You'll sleep tonight," I predicted when Laurel's head drooped.

My anxiety pricked when Nell guided her to bed. My daughter would be sleeping in the bed next to a young woman who may have murdered just a week ago. I pulled Nell back to the dining room and quietly told her what I'd heard from Nate. She scoffed at my suggestion that she sleep in the room with Annie and me and left to read in bed. I vowed to get Laurel to the police as soon as we returned to the mainland. Given the news that Marion Warfield's blood was on Laurel's clothing, I shouldn't have waited.

Annie and I cleaned up before heading to our own room, simply decorated with a cross on the wall and a figurine of the Virgin Mary on the dresser. We sat cross legged on our beds. Caesar paced back and forth between our room and Nell's until I dragged his bed to the hallway where he could watch both.

"I'm sorry I disappeared," Annie said. "I freaked out at the boarding house on Yesler. I had to get away." She closed her eyes and they moved back and forth under her pale lids reliving her fear in the hallway. It wasn't over for her.

"I owe you an apology too. I should have known that you weren't ready for that."

"I know I left abruptly, but I had to take care of myself. Grace, when I got home that night," she paused as if she wanted to stop there but went on. "As soon as I got in the door. I laid down on the floor and started shaking."

"Was it about the night Nate was shot?" I asked. "Were you—"

Annie nodded. "I couldn't stop seeing it."

"I'm so sorry, Annie." Those words were the only ones I had when there was nothing right to say. "But you are almost done. Six more months of Chaplaincy training and you'll be praying for all the patients at Harborview."

She smiled sadly, "I love the patients."

"What about until then? Would you consider seeing a therapist?" The final months of anything were always the hardest to tolerate, I was really thinking about the summons I'd received for the Calvin Cole deposition, pretty sure that she had a matching envelope from Benjamin and Beard in her mailbox. Another trigger. I decided to take care of the kitchen knives by myself and not involve her.

Annie smoothed the shiny bedspread and traced the gold roses on its quilted top. She shifted her weight and the mattress groaned. Finally, she spoke. "We used to want to be therapists, but being here is my healing, Grace."

The beds reminded me of my mother's house before I had permission to decorate my own room. My own family issues were bubbling up, but I reminded myself to hold them. I could get support from Frank. I could see the therapist.

Annie made a sound as if she wanted to speak but didn't. Caesar appeared in the doorway like he'd been called by the high emotion. He sat by Annie. The silence grew between us. I wanted to reach across the gulf between the beds, but we were both stuck in our own problems.

Finally, she found her voice. "Well."

"Well." I echoed.

"There's something I have to tell you. I'm not coming back to work." More silence. Annie sat with the bedding tented over her knees, her hands pleating the blanket. "I've decided to become a nun."

Chapter 20

Annie's bombshell was a conversation stopper. I wanted to tell her to stop, becoming a nun would be running away; instead, I gave congratulations I knew were too faint. Then, we said good night so she could sleep before her next prayers. I reached over, clicked off the lamp switch, then got up to search the kitchen for anything sharp.

A few hours later creaking floorboards from the kitchen woke me. I bolted upright and threw off the covers. Goosebumps pricked my arms, from cold air or nerves, I didn't know. The knives were under my bed, but I could have missed one. If I didn't sense a threat from Laurel, why was I so nervous? I wondered if Marion Warfield's alarms had gone off. I pulled on my jeans and went to the living room.

Laurel was wearing Frank's shirt with a white blanket over her shoulders for warmth. She'd had a bath and her hair hung clean and shiny to her shoulders. She paced the worn floor from kitchen to dining room then living room, a frantic buzzing in her throat. The counters and drawers seemed undisturbed. Laurel's face was pale, and her eyes were glazed. I filled two cups of water from the tap and gave one to her. We drank in silence. Laurel took hers in one long draw. I remembered my grandmother giving me water to drink when I was a kid and on a crying jag.

"Bad dream?" I asked.

"It's not a dream. There is blood everywhere." This sounded like a flashback, like the one Annie experienced after the evaluation on Yesler.

"Marion Warfield's blood," I stated simply. "What happened that night?" I pointed to two wooden rocking chairs in the dining room corner. "Let's sit down."

She accepted my invitation and sat and rocked. I matched the speed of my movement to hers. The motion calmed her. The chair made the same creaking noise on the floor as her pacing. It was the rhythm that brings on an alpha state, calming babies and troubled souls. Laurel would either talk or withdraw. Talking was harder. "I saw the dried blood in front of your apartment building. You were there."

She looked at me with so much intensity, I remembered that Theo had described her mother's eyes that way. "It was supposed to be a family session, but my father didn't show. Mom was the one I needed to talk to anyway. She killed a man."

"You'd just found out." I spoke.

"My grandfather told me. He said she met a boy in a bar and lost control of the situation. She slit his throat." Tears slid down her face.

"She was fourteen years old. Did he tell you about why she was in the bar?"

"Getting drunk. What else do kids do in bars?" She studied the healing red welts on her fingers. I imagined Laurel's blood mixing with Marion Warfield's.

I wanted to tell her Theo's version of the events, but this was the opening to ask about her therapist's murder. I needed the details, so I'd know how to proceed.

"Being a murderer. Can you inherit that?" Laurel's rocking stopped and she put her head in her hands.

I said softly. "What happened that night?"

"I am just like her." She seemed stuck on the thought, but eventually went on. "Mom was mad that I found out and talked about it in the family meeting. Her face got red. She said everything she did was to protect me from that."

"Then what happened?" I was afraid I'd lose her as she got closer to the memory. I wanted to hear that Mo had killed the therapist. It made sense. The method was the same.

"It was the end of the session. Marion tried to extend it, but Mom said no, she had to think. I told Mom to go—I knew she'd want to be alone. I'd be fine walking home." She put her hands over her ears. "My voices were screaming at me. I went to the bathroom on the way out. I don't know how long I was there. The lights were dimmed in the building when I finally left."

"Do you hear the voices now?"

"Yes." Her forehead creased in a frown.

Too much, too soon, I thought, and gently touched her arm to ground her.

Laurel's response was a high pitched sound from the back of her throat. Being Laurel wasn't safe right now.

"Who killed Marion Warfield?" I asked, hoping it wasn't too late.

Laurel ran her hands over the front of the shirt as if she could wipe them clean.

She took a breath and rocked. The chair still creaked, I hoped it was taking her back to a calmer space after she'd come too close to her memories. She said she was just like her mother. She'd probably already answered my question, but I needed to hear her say it.

"Did you kill Marion Warfield?"

Laurel didn't answer. I couldn't get her back to bed until after Annie tiptoed into the night for prayer with the nuns.

Chapter 21

The next morning, I missed Mass in favor of a few hours' sleep in the narrow bed. When I finally got up, Nell was in the kitchen making oatmeal. She chatted about finding almonds and coconut in the cupboard, fresh milk in a quart jar in the fridge. I looked out the window over the kitchen sink. The skies were heavy. Annie came in from Mass and we set the table, shy with each other.

"Should I call Laurel?" I asked. "She's finally asleep."

"The work will do her good," Annie said. "Then she'll sleep better tonight."

I nodded.

I could tell from her face that she saw my worry about Laurel, even as she was leaving those concerns behind.

We sat at one end of the long table and Annie gave us our assignments for *labora*. Nell and Laurel would feed the animals with her. I fought the urge to tell Annie she could have been feeding the chickens at my house if she needed that kind of labora. She assigned me to one of the nuns, a Mother Perpetua. In this order, Annie explained all the nuns were called *mother* instead of *sister*. I didn't think I needed any more mothers now, but that's what I was getting. I would meet Mother Perpetua by the herb garden. Working outside would be good for us all. I wished my grandmother had lived long enough to help at the dairy farm at Northern State Hospital.

Annie shooed me out the door so I wouldn't be late to meet with Mother Perpetua. I wandered out and saw an elderly woman with a chain saw, ready for an afternoon of work. She wasn't so bad. A beige fleece jacket complimented her coif and full-length habit, all white— none of the secular dress I saw nuns in the city wearing. Up close, she had a hawk-like nose and bright blue eyes behind wire-framed glasses. She put her hands on her hips and shook her head at the gardens at the forest edge as if they were bad children. "Look at all the blow-downs. We'll get this cleared."

Tipped alders had taken down a corner of the fence that protected the plants from browsing deer. By now all the herbs had been culled and only a few brown twigs were reminders of the bounty of basil, mint, and aromatics that must have been abuzz with bees just six weeks ago.

I offered to wield the chainsaw, but that was Mother Perpetua's territory. She handed me a pair of long-handled loppers and a pruning saw and sent me to remove all the smaller branches so she could cut the bigger pieces into firewood. I worked fast and carted the debris to a brush pile at the edge of the woods. The nun's stooped back had fooled me. She took a wide stance, and the chainsaw sliced the wood cleanly.

The whine of the chainsaw made conversation impossible, but our work was companionable. After an hour, we'd both worked up a sweat despite the crisp air and the nun shed her jacket and draped it on the garden fence.

"Mother Perpetua," I asked, "Are you named after a saint?"

She smiled. Her face was cross hatched with wrinkles and her cheeks pink from exercise. "Yes. You can call me Mother P for short. The Mother Superior chooses our names for us when we're postulants. Perpetua was an early Christian martyr. She is the patron saint of butchers too—I've always thought their need for a butcher out here had something to do with the choice."

I thought of Mo and her nose-to-tail restaurant. "You're a butcher too? You have a lot of skills."

She nodded. "I'm slowing down these days, but yes. We need old fashioned skills on the island. Most people have lost the ability to feed and care for themselves."

I nodded and admitted, "I've never really known a nun,"

"All orders are different, and I wasn't always a nun. I raised two sons before I took my vocation." She probably saw the surprise on my face. "I came after they were grown. They visit."

I liked her and decided to confide in her. "I'm worried about Annie. We worked together for years." I noticed how hard it was to put that into the past tense.

"Last week, she had a panic attack when we were evaluating a patient. She disappeared and came here." I told her about Annie's history of loss: seeing her aunt killed, witnessing Nate's shooting and how Marion Warfield's blood on the sidewalk had triggered a return of those traumas.

Mother Perpetua cocked her head as I spoke and never interrupted.

"Annie told me she wanted to become a nun and—I don't know, it's like she's running away." I heard my voice getting louder but couldn't contain it. "I don't understand much about what you do here, but I don't think you want someone running away from the outside world?"

Mother P took off her glasses and polished them. Her eyes were sunken with age, but sharp, making her seem like a bird of prey, though a friendly one.

"I understand your worry," she said. "But don't think religious life is an escape. It's harder in many ways. Grace, when a woman discerns her calling, there's no avoiding personal issues. With the Benedictines, she'll be examining all of it, much more deeply than if she stayed in the world. It's not running away. She's moving toward something, a new relationship with God, living in community." Then she replaced her glasses and focused on me. "You can see that she has been moving toward that for quite some time."

My eyes filled with the sadness I usually held at bay. "I'm afraid I haven't been open enough to hearing about her beliefs." I didn't say I was afraid of losing the partnership Annie and I'd had for years. It sounded too selfish. I liked Mother Perpetua, so I kept talking. "What about Annie's career, her education. How can she give it up?"

Mother Perpetua got a little grin on her face, that I suspected was just a step away from a laugh. "She'll find plenty of ways to use her gifts." While she waited for me to catch up with her thinking, she made an adjustment to the chain saw, preparing to get back to work.

"It's me who can't let Annie go," I finally said.

"Every woman here has had a professional life," Mother Perpetua remarked. "I practiced Clinical Psychology."

"Oh God," I said, then covered my mouth for having thoughtlessly taken the Lord's name in vain. Mother Perpetua didn't just have the wisdom of years. She had training. I'd underestimated her in every way.

"You're like family to Annie," she said. "When I first had my calling, my family and friends didn't understand but most of them tried. Not everyone stood by me though." She paused to let the words hang. Her face showed the sadness. "I still get a card every year on my birthday telling me what a terrible mistake I made. This from a woman who calls herself my friend."

My sweat had cooled during our break. I turned to raking and stacking the wood while Mother Perpetua cut the white, dappled alders to uniform lengths. Behind her the Douglas Fir began to sway and toss their boughs in a new wind. The sky was foreboding, and I pictured a new round of blowdowns.

"Oh no," I said. "All our work is about to be undone."

Mother Perpetua paused in gathering up the tools and gave a smile that made me feel understood. Her eyes showed the universal cycle of doing and undoing that I struggled against. I knew there was a lot I could learn here, but that was Annie's path, not mine.

"That's enough for today," my *labora* companion said. "You really should come to prayers before you leave."

The next prayer was at three, pushing our trip back to Seattle a bit later. On my way back to the guest house, the tang of saltwater from the straits mixed with the freshly cut wood carried on the wind. It was invigorating and not strong enough to make me worry. The closeness of nature reminded me of home. Maybe that was part of the appeal for Annie. Maybe planting a climbing vine in the window where she lost the view wasn't enough. Talking to Mother Perpetua had helped me. Annie had known what she was doing when she assigned us to work together. She had sent me to the therapist.

Inside, the house was warm. Annie and Nell sat in the rocking chairs talking with the dog at their feet. "We took Caesar for a run in the woods, away from all the farm animals," Annie said. She knew he didn't have a good history with our chickens.

I pulled a dining room chair to join them. "Thanks. You know Annie, I really liked working with Mother Perpetua."

She smiled.

"Where's Laurel?"

"In the tub," Nell said.

We ate leftover stew and set a bowl aside so Laurel could take her time. When she finally emerged, she and Nell decided they'd miss None, the 3:00 prayer, in favor of making sandwiches for the trip home. I gave Nell the bread knife from my secret stash, figuring that it would be safe with supervision. Laurel had taken her medication and was calmer after a morning caring for the animals.

Annie stood up. "Let's leave early for None. We can talk."

We headed up the gravel road with the dark forest on our left.

I took a deep breath and struggled to find the words. "I don't think I ever accepted how deep your religious beliefs were. I still don't think I understand, but I'll try."

"Do you want to talk about it now?" Annie asked.

"I've softened, but I don't think this is the moment."

"Lord make me pure, but not yet."

"What?"

"It's a quote from St. Augustine when he wasn't quite ready to become chaste—not to compare you to a saint, Grace."

"Saint jokes," I said. "Who knew."

Annie gave a deep, relaxed laugh like I hadn't heard from her in quite a while.

The chapel's setting was carved out of the forest. It had an Asian design fronted by Japanese maples and chunks of granite. The effect was spare and calm.

"The nuns live there," Annie waved to the left. If the chapel was public, their space was truly enclosed, fronted by a stacked wall of wood rounds that had turned mossy and become one with the woodland. Skinny saplings grew on top with slender roots searching the face for purchase. We passed that enclosure and stood outside the church, a few minutes early for the service.

"I need to fill you in on Laurel." It was my last chance to tell Annie about my concerns: that the blood on Laurel's clothing belonged to the therapist, that Mo had killed a man when she was young, and that the knives were hidden under my bed in the guesthouse.

"Oh yes—you really should have called the police." Annie put her hands on her hips. "But I still say if you keep digging, you'll prove that Laurel didn't do it."

"I'll do that when she is in a safe place." I felt powerless to do anything better. "There's something else. There's going to be a deposition for Calvin Cole's trial. I'm afraid you've got a letter from the attorneys in your mail too."

There was the trigger. Annie's calm mood faltered. "When is it?"

"I've been called for the day after tomorrow. I'm dreading it."

Her healthy glow dimmed. "I've done these before, but still. This case is different." Our breathing and the wind were the only sounds in the clearing, but I saw the nuns, now dressed in black, quietly processing in the back door of the chapel. "I'll give you my keys when you leave today so you check my mail."

"Okay."

"If I've been called, will you stay with me when I give my statement?"

I reached for her hand. "If they'll let me—of course," I said. This was the sort of thing I was good at.

Inside, the chapel continued the calmness of Asian design, but when we took a place in the pews, I was taken aback to see the nuns file in behind the altar, separated from the other worshippers by a wooden half-wall topped by balusters. I couldn't help but see the gulf coming between me and Annie when it was expressed so physically—she would be walled off. Mother Perpetua had said that all orders were different, and in this holy place, I silently cursed Annie for choosing one that seemed so isolated.

The nuns were all elderly like Mother Perpetua and sang the Latin chants in high wavering voices. Annie's voice was younger and clearer, she held the prayer book so I could join, but I whispered that I would rather listen.

After the service, we mingled in the courtyard brightened by the colors of October leaves. I thanked Mother Perpetua and, even with my misgivings, told her I was beginning to accept that Annie would be leaving Seattle for the island.

Her eyes took on a concerned look. "Not for long, though dear. Annie will be going to our mother house on the east coast."

I looked at Annie wondering why she hadn't told me that herself. She just nodded. We walked back to the guesthouse without saying much. I wouldn't know where to begin. Inside, Nell and Laurel leaned forward in the rocking chairs locked in a conversation that stopped when we appeared.

"Tell her," Nell said.

Laurel didn't say a word. She let the chair rock back, so she was straight. She didn't look scared or preoccupied. She seemed the most focused I'd seen her.

Annie and I dragged straight-backed chairs from the table and made a circle.

"What?" I asked.

After a moment, Laurel rocked forward again. "I am not going back to Seattle."

"Where do you want to go?" I asked. "Not back to your Grandfather's."

"No. I'm staying here."

Annie took over then, explaining that the nuns would soon be shutting down the guesthouse for the season. "I'll be leaving too."

Laurel crossed her arms in front of her. She looked like a stubborn kid. "I'm staying. I'm safe here."

I thought about what awaited her back in the city. Did she sense that she'd be returned to the hospital, or sent to Western State or jail? I could see why she wanted to stay. Annie continued to talk to Laurel in a calm, reassuring voice, but didn't make any progress in convincing her. Then I saw Annie lean away from the power struggle. "Grace and I are going to walk the dog and talk for a few minutes."

Outside, the color had drained from the day. The low clouds, the pasture, the forest, everything looked gray.

"I can't pick Laurel up and carry her," I said.

Annie and I walked along the wire fence and the long-horned cattle joined us, exciting Caesar. He trembled at the end of his leash.

"I guess I'll call the police then," Annie said.

"They'll come over on the ferry?"

Annie looked to the heavens in response. "This is Island County. I'm pretty sure the police have a boat." She walked up the hill where she could get cell service to make the calls.

Chapter 22

On the ferry back to Anacortes, I watched Shaw Island, and Annie, recede in the darkening waters. The sun broke through the clouds leaving a halo of light, a kind of holy isolation. I was glad to leave the problem of Laurel with Annie, just as glad as I was to leave my grandmother at Northern State Hospital. I needed a break but driving south on I-5 while Nell napped gave me too much time to think.

The memory that had been nagging me began to fill in. It was the summer I turned 10. That summer my mother had tried to commit suicide. I had been at my grandparents, outside playing and came in the back, proud that I'd remembered to close the door quietly, so quietly that my grandparents didn't hear me. My grandmother was hanging her cleaning rags up to dry and my grandfather stood with his arms crossed.

"What if Grace had been with her?"

I'd already overheard a phone call that she'd taken too many pills. We didn't talk about it.

"Rose planned it when she'd be here. I'm sure of it."

"Well then," he said. "Grace should stay with us. We'll put her in school and that's that. Just like we did with Rose."

The colors in the room went bright. I would get to stay here where meals were on the table at six, clothes were washed and ironed, and life was always summer vacation.

"I can stay?" I asked from the doorway, relieved. Guilty.

My grandmother turned woodenly, looking from my grandfather to me and back. "Your mother is going to be just fine." I'd never seen her look so stricken.

I was back with Mom in September, as usual. Struggling with thoughts that my mother had tried to leave me, and my grandmother didn't want to take me in.

Picking up Annie's mail added an extra half hour to the trip home. Then Nell took over driving, I nodded off on I-90 eastbound. We were winding the hairpin curve before our house when I woke up. There were no streetlights beyond town and the night was as dark as on the island. If Annie found Our Lady of the Rock a place for her healing, this was mine. The windows across the back of our house were lit a warm yellow. Even on our worst days, Frank and Nell were a comfort.

Caesar was overjoyed to be home and ran circles around the orchard sniffing out any new visitors to his territory. Frank was in the kitchen browning garlic for our favorite pasta with tuna and olives. A fire crackled in the living room woodstove. Frank washed his hands and hugged us both. Before Nell stowed our duffle bags, she set Grandma Lucy's suitcase from the state hospital in a place of honor before the fire. I cringed, wanting some respite from the family drama.

After the long ride, I was glad to make a salad and set the table. Nell caught Frank up on the news about Laurel and Annie. "I spent a lot of time with Laurel so Mom could talk to Annie—with her *I'm going to be a nun,* bombshell."

Frank poured each of us a glass of Sangiovese. "The nuns in my school were scary, except for Sister Claudette, I'd have done anything for her."

"I know what you mean," I said. "A day clearing brush with Mother Perpetua is probably as good as a month of therapy. Annie will be like that." She always had been, that's why I loved working with her. My real problem was that my friend, and daughter, were following paths that led them so far away.

Nell arranged a tray to carry the wine and hors d'oeuvres into the living room while the sauce bubbled, but she hesitated at the kitchen table and echoed my thoughts. "Spending time with Annie was like that for me too. I'm glad after what happened with my boss."

Frank and I waited. Nell had avoided talking about this until now and the words still weren't coming easily. "Did you talk about the harassment with Annie?" I finally asked.

She nodded, then looked up with more than a little defiance. "She helped me see that I was blaming myself. I thought I didn't belong as an interpreter in the first place and maybe I don't. I'm not a native speaker so how could I be good enough? Then I had time to think even more on the drive home. My supervisor preyed on that doubt. I am going into town tomorrow to file a complaint with the director of the agency."

"Good for you." I said softly. Nell didn't like feeling over-encouraged when she made decisions.

She shrugged. "I don't know if it will go anywhere, especially if I'm out of the country, but maybe I can do whatever follow up they need by email. I still feel like it's small. Worse things happen to women all the time."

"It's small because you got out. If you had agreed to have sex in return for your job, it would have grown much larger. Speaking up helps all the women who experience worse. You are part of the wave."

Nell looked taller and more at ease when she carried the tray into the living room, and we took our favorite seats around the fire. The only thing that marred the mood was the leather-trimmed suitcase blocking the warmth. I didn't know what to make of it.

Nell noticed my gaze. "Sexual harassment is like the stigma of mental illness. There has been too much silence around them both."

I regarded the suitcase with a mixture guilt and irritability. "I feel like I've brought contraband into the house."

Frank agreed. "I remember when I first met your grandparents. They were warm and welcoming, but one day I asked about when they adopted your mom. The silence was stunning. You whispered that you'd tell me later."

"You're right," I said. "Grandma Lucy was unspeakable, but I didn't know why."

My grandparents and their home here in Duvall were the best part in my childhood. But even after all the good they did by taking my mother when Lucy was hospitalized at Northern State, an old sadness weighed on my chest. Their silence had hurt my mother in her own struggle with depression. I thought about Mom's inability to talk about what happened. The rational part of me understood that silence was the way almost everyone of that era handled mental illness, especially in small towns where people might talk and judge, but it would have helped me to know.

Caesar noticed our focus on the suitcase. He left his spot at my feet and walked toward it and stopped short with his ruff up. My sentiments exactly.

"They watched me take up my career in mental health," I said. "They never asked me about my work and never told me about my Grandma Lucy's illness. I've talked to hundreds of families over the years when their loved ones became ill. I talk about understanding the symptoms and..." I threw up my hands in frustration and stared at in the suitcase. Caesar lowered his head and barked at it. He didn't stop when I tried to quiet him.

Nell put a finger to her lips. "I don't know if you believe in ghosts, but Grandma and Grandpa Winters aren't ready for this. Even Caesar knows." She picked up the old suitcase and carried it to the front closet. "There's no key anyway. We can save it for another day. At least we know it's here."

I felt as if an atmospheric pressure had lifted from the room. Caesar curled up in his bed and we laughed at the truth and absurdity of what Nell had said—My grandparents still didn't want to talk about it.

"Let's eat," Frank said. The smell of the sauce wafting from the kitchen told us the dinner was almost ready.

After we ate, I delivered the dirty plates to the sink and Frank washed. I wiped the crumbs from the dark oak table into my palm then gave up and swept them off the edge. The floors were my job and I'd been remiss. The old vinyl was a brick pattern that had been here since I was a kid. Now it was coated in mud from

Caesar's paws and drifts of fur from autumn shedding. The spot under Frank's feet at the sink had worn to a layer of black backing.

I grabbed the broom and started sweeping. "My grandmother would never have let the floor get this bad. It used to sparkle. She was always waxing it."

Frank gave me a strange look. "I seem to remember that's why she wouldn't have a dog in the house. No chance of avoiding dirt with Caesar."

The dog just followed the broom looking for crumbs. I worked my way over to the built-in desk and the paper bag filled with Annie's mail. "Oh no, I forgot this."

I abandoned sweeping and tilted the bag, spilling the contents onto the desktop and sorted flyers and obvious junk from the real mail. Halfway down, I found the attorneys' envelope and ripped it open—Annie's appointment, just like mine, read October 30, the day after tomorrow. She would have to leave in the morning to be back in time. I decided to call right away. She'd be checking in and would probably walk up the hill toward better reception around prayer time. I left a short message with the details about our check-in time at the attorneys' downtown offices and my phone rang as soon as I hung up. The screen read Annie.

I said hi and started to mention the date again, but she cut me off.

"I'll be there," she said, her voice tight. "But that's not why I'm calling. Laurel is gone."

I almost laughed with surprise, but it wasn't funny. "How?"

"I was waiting for the police but figured going to Vespers would be okay. Where could she go? It's an island. When I came back, Laurel was nowhere to be found. Mother Perpetua and I organized a search party for the roads and trails. What if she'd been wandering in the woods? Nights are cold. But when I went back to the guest house, the donations box was gone."

"Oh no. I left plenty of money. She'd be able to get back to the mainland and then some."

"Exactly," Annie said. "We got to the ferry terminal before the last run. There aren't many walk-ons, so the guy remembered her.

She must have hitchhiked that far. The police boat arrived when we were at the terminal. Too late."

"Where do you think she would go? Surely not to her grandfathers' house. To her apartment? Her mother's house?"

"One of those," Annie said.

I wasn't so sure. "She's slippery. The locked psych unit couldn't hold her, and neither could an island. Last time she went to her father. Oh man, here we go again. Searching for Laurel."

"There's one piece of good news," Annie said before signing off. "Looks like she took her medications with her."

Chapter 23

I was responsible for losing Laurel. I should have dealt with this at her grandfather's house and waited for the local authorities. Now I had to call Nate. He picked up right away.

"I'm sorry." What else could I say? I explained that I'd gotten his message about Marion Warfield's blood on Laurel's clothing—after the ferry left dock.

"God, Grace." His voice was frustrated. "I wanted you to leave this to the police, but you're two steps ahead of them anyway."

I told Nate how to find Laurel's father and grandfather. I told him about Theo. "He said Mo killed his brother and I believe him." I told him I thought it was Mo who killed Marion Warfield, though I couldn't rule out Laurel.

Nate promised to talk to the detectives.

I woke the next morning and knew I needed to follow my instincts. I had to talk to Mo. I dialed her number. Laurel was gone again, disappeared from both the hospital and the island. Running from a legacy of murder.

"Have you heard from Laurel?" I asked as soon as Mo picked up the phone. The question sounded normal, as far as Mo knew, her daughter had never been found.

"No. But today, that's good," she said, her voice was tight, and her words clipped. "I'm afraid."

"What happened?"

"Someone's been following me for a long time. It's still happening. I've been threatened."

"Threatened?"

"I'm sure it's the man you saw."

"Theo Martinez," I said.

A long silence followed as Mo took in that I knew his name and probably more.

Finally, she said, "Come to the restaurant. We need to talk."

Of course, I said yes. I'd leave right away and stop on my way to work. I let Caesar out the backdoor so he could run while I put on a skirt and a purple knit top still warm from the drier. I zipped up my knee-high boots to make me feel strong.

It wasn't until the Prius was idling at the stop sign at Cherry Valley Road, that I remembered that the Elegant Beast was, except for Sunday Brunch, open only at dinner. I didn't want to be alone with Mo James. The weather report threatened rain, but it hadn't arrived. The sky was an unbroken gray like a lid on the valley. I would ask Mo to meet me in public, the same way I stayed safe on blind dates of my youth. My stomach was in knots.

I knocked on the beveled glass door of the Elegant Beast. Mo's face appeared right away, but she didn't suggest I come in. She slid out the front door and pulled it closed behind her. Her platinum hair was flat on one side and a splatter of something brown had congealed on her white chef's coat.

"I have something to show you," she said and motioned me toward the end of the block.

I bristled at her directive. I was finally realizing I couldn't help this family.

I followed her to the alley behind the building where I had seen Theo watching on the night of the homeless count. This area was isolated too. The river trail behind us was empty. At the back door of the Beast, Mo pointed. There, nailed to the pale green doorframe was a dead squirrel, stiffened legs splayed, head pointing toward the ground. Rusty colored blood from the head had dripped down the frame and dried. The implied violence made me sweat in the cool air.

Mo spoke. "You saw the man who was watching. Theo Martinez did this."

I didn't think Theo did it, but I was confused about who did.

"I found it this morning," Mo said.

The fur was matted with blood and the body stiff. It reminded me of the squirrel by the trailer at Patrick's ramshackle house. Mo's father.

"This is terrible," I said. "but you need the police, not me. I don't know how to help."

"I called the police. Their response? They said it was probably done by a disgruntled vegetarian protesting my menu."

I hugged myself for warmth on the dank back stoop of the restaurant. "This isn't the work of someone who avoids killing animals," I said. The doorframe with the squirrel was painted a new and shiny green, a shade lighter than the moss on the cedar shingles.

"I'm afraid he'll kill me," she said simply. Mo also wrapped her arms around herself, like she could hold herself together.

"I don't know how I can help," I said again.

"I know you're looking for Laurel. If you find her. Keep her away."

This was when I should have told Mo that I had found, and lost Laurel again. I didn't.

It was possible someone was telling her they knew her secret. She had killed. For now, I led Mo away from whatever the squirrel was meant to symbolize. I kept my hand gently on her arm, so she was ahead of me and guided her out of the isolated alley. Her body coiled with emotion and I wanted her in a neutral place where I had planned to speak with her—a coffee shop across Main Street. We walked up the hill to the corner, but our paths were blocked.

Costumed children from toddlers to teens rushed from store to store to fill their bags with candy. Halloween was two days away, but the schools had planned the annual costume parade for this morning. A tall white chicken with trouble seeing out of its beak careened into us. A knot of princesses followed superheroes with muscular padded costumes. Two crows with cartoon faces flapped by. We wove through the masquerading children to get to the Grateful Bread Cafe. I noticed that witches, demons, and the dark side were missing from this Halloween. Even the crows looked benign, not like the birds that pick the bones of the dead. I envied their innocence.

I looked at Mo James, disheveled and tense, trying to cross the street. Had her own father threatened her? This was not a happy family. She had recreated herself, but that was fraying now.

Inside, we found a table in back and draped our jackets on the chairs. The shop smelled of dark roast coffee and scones. Mo paid for the Americano I didn't feel like drinking and carried the cups to the table. She carefully set them down and lowered herself into the chair. Then she leaned forward to grasp my hand. Even after holding the cups, her touch was cold as if her body had drawn all her energy to her core. Whatever threats she received; she had drawn them to her. I suspected she had killed again, and I planned to find out what happened the night Marion was murdered. The espresso machine hissed.

"I met the man who was watching that night," I said. "His name is Theo Martinez.

She withdrew into her chair and after a long while answered, "Yes," in a controlled voice. "How do you know his name? What did he tell you?"

"Are you afraid he will threaten you or expose you?"

Her answer was vague. "He's the man who followed me for twenty years."

"You killed his brother," I said quietly.

After a few moments, she said, "Yes," and seemed to relax into her chair. Her face showed no emotion: no anger, no sadness and now, not even the fear she'd been carrying.

I couldn't read her. No matter what Annie said about our ability to trust gut reactions and know things, I really had no idea. I didn't know what she had done. I didn't even know if she had put the squirrel on the door frame herself. I did believe Theo.

"I don't think he's dangerous," I said, "But he wants some justice."

"Justice?" She asked with a bitter laugh. "I went upstairs with his brother. I was a kid."

"So was his brother."

"But older and bigger. And much drunker. I tried to say no. I said I didn't want to have sex."

I thought of Nell, but this was different. "Start over. Theo showed me a newspaper clipping that traced you and your father around rural Washington State. The two of you ran a scam. Sex with you was the prize."

"No." She shook her head emphatically. "The *promise* of sex with me was the prize. I always managed to get out of it and make off with their wallets and watches too. I was a thief not a whore. A fourteen-year-old thief. This guy pulled his knife. I was smart. I got flirtatious and made suggestive jokes about opening his blade. He set the knife down thinking he'd get what he wanted. I grabbed it."

I could nearly picture the saloon, the dark room upstairs, but what I heard was the thunk of the barista knocking the grounds from the filter handle.

Mo kept her voice low and private from the other patrons. "He struggled to get it back and I panicked. He could easily have overpowered me, but I've always been very fast, and I'd been hunting and butchering since I was twelve. I slit his throat and ran."

"You were fourteen," I said, now empathy for her washed over me. I wasn't sure the feeling was useful, but I'd met Mo's father and had a sense of his grooming young girls.

"What I told you about no mental health history in the family wasn't exactly true," she said. "My father never had a diagnosis, but you would call him grandiose. He couldn't manage life. My mom took off when I was ten and left us kids with him. I was the oldest and tried to look out for the younger ones. He didn't work. I did the scams so we could eat. To feed the younger kids. My whole life was about feeding people. It still is."

"Theo wouldn't nail a squirrel to your door," I said.

"He would." Neither of us had touched our coffees.

I waited.

"When we got to that bar, my father hadn't chosen who the mark would be. I was talking to Theo. I told him how I'd learned to hunt when I was younger. Squirrel. And how it horrified me. I didn't tell him why. The day I shot my first squirrel my father smeared the blood on my face and told me it was a rite of passage. It was also the day I had my first period. I had no mother to tell me anything. I thought I was dying."

"I'm sorry," I tried to imagine Theo using that information against her now, but the picture I came up with was of the father she had broken with so many years earlier.

Mo shrugged and almost managed to look nonchalant. "It made me tough. I put it behind me. I can do everything except keep my daughter safe."

I wondered what Mo would do, imaging she was keeping Laurel safe. Would she kill a therapist who encouraged Laurel to learn about her past? Marion Warfield was killed in the same way Angel Martinez' was, and the police had only reported a stabbing.

"You never told Laurel about your father or the scam," I said.

"I gave her the normal life I never had. It worked until now."

"It never works," I said. "Kids read the undercurrents. Laurel told me that she killed her therapist. She thinks she followed in your footsteps. Unless you killed Marion Warfield."

Mo leaned forward and said an emphatic, "No." He face was red and her hands tightened into fists.

"Your secrets have done nothing but hurt Laurel. How far did you go to keep that secret? Did you kill her therapist?"

"No," she said again.

"Tell me what really happened." I ventured.

"I did." She affirmed. "You're wrong. There's nothing else to tell."

I didn't believe her. The problem was that Marion Warfield's blood had been found on Laurel's clothing, not her mother's.

When I left the coffee shop only a few trick or treaters remained. Some looked about high school age by their size. They shoved each other a little too hard. One costume was gray fur with a long upright tail. When the boy turned, I saw a squirrel. White face and belly, long teeth, and whiskers. Molded eyes and nose. For a moment, I thought it had to do with Mo. Then, the reveler reached up and struggled with the head and pulled it off. He might have been a football player with a broad neck and sweet eyes. He laughed with his friends.

Chapter 24

My commute gave me time to think. I had no enthusiasm for returning to work. The story of Laurel's family was like a Greek tragedy—people controlled by a fate they can't seem to change. I drove west on the 520 bridge because the lighted reader board told me it would be 3 minutes faster getting into the city. The only good thing about work was that for the next eight hours, I'd be focused on something else. It was better than meditation.

In our afternoon meeting, I was assigned to do evaluations in the hospital. Annie's old role. I'd be inside seeing a man on a medical unit who had jumped from a 4th floor window. But first, I had someone in the psychiatric emergency service, Victor, the young Russian I'd seen the night I evaluated Laurel. He'd already been discharged from the hospital and had returned since then.

"Miss Grace!" Victor greeted me with the usual fist bump and expansive speech. His curly blond hair was a tangled halo around his head, and he wore the hospital-issue, snap fronted pajamas, which probably meant he'd been disrobing in public again.

"What happened? I didn't expect to see you so soon." Sometimes a good outcome is for people to have longer spaces between hospitalizations.

He lowered his voice, "It's the KGB. They told me things I must tell the president. I must get to him. Putin is my father. He will never..."

"You must be worried," I responded and tried to redirect him. "Why did the police bring you here?"

"I was in the Starbucks. No one would listen so I..." He grasped the front of his pajama top and was about to rip it open.

"I know the Russian protest," I laughed. "I've seen it all."

"So, you have, but I must tell the president."

I gave him my best *I'm listening* nod. "Word to the wise, though. Don't try to contact the president. If the secret service—it doesn't matter if they are right or wrong—thinks you could get to the president and might be a danger, you'll go to federal lockup, not Harborview."

Victor considered this. "I like you, Miss Grace. Do you remember the first time we met?"

I did. "You were still living with your family in Kent. How long has it been? Ten years?"

"Yes! We had just moved here. We were persecuted in Russia because we are Jehovah's Witness, a religion they don't like. They followed us and called us extremist. They say we are dangerous. Why? Because we tell others about our religion. My family knew people in Washington state, so we came."

I nodded, thinking about the difficulties of religion and religious people who weren't respected. Yet a thing humanity had been drawn to since the beginning of time. Except for me. I was guilty of not respecting Annie's beliefs.

Victor continued. "I don't care if no one believes like me. People say I'm crazy. But you Miss Grace, you listen. You write the court order and force me stay in the hospital, but you know me, and you don't disrespect me."

If only I could do as well in my personal life. "Thank you," I told him sincerely. Sometimes I thought this was the best I could do in my job—to listen to people who were usually ignored.

Victor jumped out of the plastic chair so fast he had to reach to keep it upright. "Are you religious? No wait. You're going to tell me you don't discuss your religion. I know you." He waved his hand expansively to take in the brightly lit hallway. "This is your church. I tell people about Jehovah and you listen to people the world thinks are crazy then send them to the hospital."

I laughed and looked around. "Maybe you're right, but enough about me. That's not what I'm here to talk about today."

Then, I politely directed our talk back to Victor's symptoms and the behavior that led to his being sent to the hospital.

When I finished talking to him, I gave him a final fist bump. Heading back to the office, I passed the tiny room where I had first met Laurel and her mother. In a strange twist on the Sins-of-the-Fathers story, Laurel may have re-enacted the murder committed by her mother. At least she thought she had.

I took the elevator to the 4th floor orthopedic ward where the man who had jumped from the window was recuperating with one leg in traction. A person with ongoing suicidal ideation was difficult to deal with on a medical unit. They had to hire a Hospital Assistant to sit with him 24 hours a day to assure his safety. The psychiatric units were designed for that: safety windows behind heavy locked screens, no sharps, no cords that could be wrapped around a neck. Not so the medical units.

At the nurses' station, a woman with blue hair and pink scrubs said, "You here to see the jumper?"

"Marshall Logan," I read from the intake sheet to give him a name so he wouldn't be identified by his action alone.

She led me to Room 432, a double. Mr. Logan's bed was by the window, separated from his roommate by a light green curtain. I was about to nod and say, "Good evening," as I passed, but I stopped abruptly. The man in the first bed was asleep. It was Emery Warfield, also with a leg in traction.

"Just a minute," I said to the nurse and stepped back out of the room. "I know that man."

"You do?" she said. "He's a John Doe. Came in all broken up. Hit and run while he was walking down the sidewalk. Can you believe it? No ID on him and he's unconscious."

I looked in at Marion Warfield's brother. His sandy hair had turned the pillow brown from dirt. An IV snaked into his arm and an oxygen cannula hissed in his nose. I wished I could talk to him about his sister, but he was unmoving. "His sister just died. I met him at the memorial." A wave of sadness hit me because sometimes bad things keep happening to the same people. Emery Warfield was one. "How do I go about reporting his name?"

"I'll help you call the Admitting Office when you're done," the nurse responded.

Before I went to introduce myself to Marshall Logan and do my assessment, my phone vibrated in my pocket. Nate again. He was keeping me in the loop.

"I'll tell you what I heard," he said. "They found Marion Warfield's car parked in front of the girl's apartment. The university was resurfacing the garage she used. At first the detectives thought it was ominous that Warfield was there after the session, but it was only parking."

"Try to see it through Laurel's eyes though," I said. "She must have found it ominous. Her therapist dressed in black, seeming to follow her home. What else?"

"Warfield's purse was found in a dumpster right there. No phone. No wallet. One more thing. Warfield apparently has a brother. He looks homeless and hard to find."

"I can help there," I said and told him about Emery Warfield on 4E.

After I finished my evaluation on the roommate, I glanced out the window at the night sky. The city sparkled with lights and I longed to be outside in the cool air. Instead, I stopped by Emery's bed and sat in the molded plastic chair, watching his chest rise and fall. "I'm sorry this happened to you," I said, being a firm believer that on some level, people who are unconscious can at least sense a supportive presence. "And I'm going to find the person who killed your sister." His breath seemed to catch, or maybe it was my imagination. I sat quietly for another minute and said, "I think I'm close." I wanted to give both of us hope.

In the morning, after not enough sleep, I was crossing the floating bridge again—to the attorney's office downtown. A steady breeze from the north leaned into the bridge and made the water on Lake Washington choppy. I was glad this was only a deposition—no courthouse, no jury, no cross examination, and no sense. Why were we being called for testimony on an evaluation that we hadn't attended? Courts were sticklers for hearing what was seen or heard. Annie and I hadn't been there.

I was scheduled for 8:30 and Annie was later in the morning. The attorney hadn't been pleased when I'd asked to be with Annie to support her, but she said yes, I could sit in the room as long as I didn't interfere. I'd have finished my statement, so hearing Annie couldn't sway me.

The Benjamin and Beard Law Group was on the 10th floor of a glass building on 3rd Avenue near the courthouse. I stopped in the bathroom on the way, to brush my hair back into a professional looking knot. At my right temple, threads of gray seemed to have appeared overnight. I plucked them out with my fingers and dotted concealer on the dark circles under my eyes.

Brene Benjamin, with her coifed blond hair and polka dot dress under a navy-blue jacket, looked like she could play a lawyer on television except for the scuffed UGGs on her feet. She directed me to a conference room with a wall of windows overlooking Puget Sound and deposited me with her intern, Sammy, a young man with a little mustache and slick black hair, who would run me through pre-deposition coaching and filming. It felt like they wanted acting more than truth. This law group was representing the hospital which, of course, hoped to settle out of court.

Sammy adjusted the camera and began the rehearsal questioning. He directed me to a white board. "Please draw the layout of the Cole residence."

I drew a square with the front door where Annie and I entered. The living room to the left. I saw the Cole parents standing by their recliners. The narrow hallway. I saw Nate fall and felt Mrs. Cole's shoe strike me as she ran to her son. My heart raced and my field of vision narrowed.

"We'll come back to that in a moment," the intern said.

I closed my eyes and steadied myself.

"What information did you receive about Mr. Calvin Cole's alcohol intake before entering the residence?"

He had a copy of the intake form too, but he wanted me to read it for the recording. The paper rattled in my hands when I paged to the information. I was still seeing the Cole house. "Occasional alcohol use. Two or three beers several times a week."

"Was there any report of threats to the family in your pre-visit paperwork?"

I saw where this was going, the firm wanted to discredit the family. Make it seem like they withheld information from Annie and me. Also, from the doctor who evaluated him the day before. Maybe they did, whether from their inexperience with the system, fear of stigma, or poor interviewing by the phone contact.

"No threats were reported, but this document was completed several hours before I arrived."

"Please answer only the question asked. Yes or no."

"No," I said tersely. I was familiar with court procedure but irritated by it too.

He went on to ask about weapons.

"None known," I read.

"But there was a weapon."

"Yes, but I don't know if the family was aware..." I focused on my words, but I saw the weapon flash.

The intern turned off the camera. "Ms. Vaccaro, yes or no only."

"I can't do this anymore." I didn't try to hide my feelings now that I wasn't being filmed. I stood up and walked to the window. The Bainbridge Ferry left the Coleman Dock opening a V in the still water behind it. A seagull swooped toward the glass window. I glanced down to see it chase a blue-gray pigeon from a ledge where it tried to shelter.

"What outcome do you want here, ma'am?"

I turned back to the sterile, but expensively furnished room. Was I supposed to help the hospital? I just wanted justice; a concept so unlikely it had made Mo James laugh. The family wanted more money, the hospital wanted to pay less. Calvin Cole certainly did need treatment, probably more than he could access.

"I just want Calvin Cole to have the care and treatment he deserves. It's all I ever want."

"Well, you're going to have to pull yourself together." Sammy said and scratched his Clark Gable mustache. I knew he saw my upset, but he just reminded me of the rules before restarting the film. He wasn't about to deal with my intrusive memories or idealism. I dug my fingernails into my palms until the sharpness helped me face the next two hours of questions.

Sammy, the intern got a break after that and Annie's session was led by Brene Benjamin. It was much shorter. I sat in a row of chairs against the wall while Annie took her place at the conference table. She wore a soft, rust colored sweater that looked like cashmere and made me wonder who would get her hand-me-downs when she moved to the convent.

There was no need for another drawing of the Cole house or half the questions I'd answered. I was glad for her sake. Annie sailed through calmly and we were out by lunchtime.

The weak October sun had fled, replaced by threatening clouds in the west. Downtown workers flowed around us, looking for lunch. Annie and I stood in front of the glass tower saying good-bye. I felt restless and out of sorts after my morning with Sammy, the intern. Now I needed to find out who killed Marion Warfield—even if it turned out to be Laurel.

"I'm going to walk up to Harborview. My car's there and Marion Warfield's brother is on the Orthopedic Unit." I told Annie about seeing him yesterday.

Annie zipped her parka. She looked okay, more confident than she'd been in months. "I'll come with you," she said. "How was your deposition?"

"Grueling. I want to put the whole Calvin Cole mess behind me," I said. Unfortunately, everything ahead was messy too, including our friendship. "Annie, I was imagining taking the ferry to visit you on the island, but Mother Perpetua told me you'd be moving back East to the main convent. Why didn't you tell me?"

"I guess I didn't think you could handle it," Annie answered.

"Not handle it?" I bristled. "I handle things."

A wind from Puget Sound funneled between the buildings on James Street. An empty sandwich wrapper blew into my legs and stayed, held by the wind.

"Look at your last two years. Your neighbor was murdered. Nate was shot. Your mom died. You handle things too much. You know it adds up."

"What can I do but handle it?" I said. She hadn't even mentioned that both she and Nell would be leaving. I finally told her about how the deposition had affected me.

Annie frowned at my distress. "Mr. Intern was an asshole."

I loved it when Annie swore and smiled weakly, with the confusion that hit me when my well-honed defenses were stripped away. I reached down and ripped the checkered sandwich wrapper that was still plastered to my pants leg by the wind. A smear of mustard stuck to my hand and I searched my bag for a tissue.

"Oh man, Grace. You act so tough; I actually fall for it." Annie came closer. Her arm went around me, and I leaned my head on her shoulder.

If I had planned the perfect way to help Annie on a day with the potential to trigger her past trauma, it would be for me to need support. Trading coping skills with Annie wasn't going to work for me though. I pointed toward the hospital. We had the walk sign, and we ran across Third Avenue before the light turned. Part way up the hill, she stopped. We were already breathing hard. James Street was on a hill so steep that cars with a clutch drove blocks to avoid it.

"There's one more thing I haven't told you. I knew Marion Warfield, before." Annie's cheeks were red from exertion mixed with a little shame at having withheld this. "When I worked with kids at the Adolescent Center in Burien, I was her social worker. She was one of the sickest kids I knew. Her manic symptoms were intense."

"I figured that out already." I said, picturing the accomplished-looking Marion I'd seen in pictures as an acting-out teen. Then I remembered Annie, so sick in her apartment after we learned Marion had been murdered. Annie had more secrets than I'd realized. "Why didn't you tell me?"

"I couldn't process it. She was so special. She got better. I didn't want to tarnish her memory. I was going to tell you," Annie paused. "Later."

"After you reconnected with her at SU. She must have been having symptoms there."

Annie shrugged and took a few more steps up the hill. "We can see that now, but she managed her work life beautifully. She seemed to be the success story we could only dream of." Her eyes were full of tears. I could see how deeply Marion Warfield's death had struck her. We started up hill again. It wasn't conducive to talking and I tried to make sense of this new information.

"I was no good with adolescents. You've got to be cool, or they won't trust you. Or good at sports," Annie said. "Marion was the only part of that job I liked. She was wild."

"You were always good at the wild stuff."

"Better than basketball anyway, but not anymore."

"Marion's death must have broken your heart," I said.

Annie stopped in the middle of the sidewalk and we looked up the steep hill in front of us. It seemed such a long way.

Chapter 25

We entered the hospital and took the elevator to the orthopedic floor. The white board at the nurses' station showed that Emery Warfield was in the same room. I led the way around the circular unit to his room. By now his roommate had moved to the psychiatric unit. The second bed was empty and clean.

Emery lay against the fresh white bedding, eyes closed, his tanned skin slack on high cheek bones. I remembered him at the memorial and saw the photo of him boating with his sister at Lake Burien. He now was either asleep or still unconscious. Numerous tubes connected him to blinking machines. We quietly moved two chairs to the bedside. Annie sat and closed her eyes; her lips moved in silent prayer. I tiptoed out and learned from the nurse that he had not yet awakened.

I rejoined Annie and gave her the news. She gently put her hand on his arm and began to talk as if he could hear. "I remember meeting you once, years ago. I was Marion's social worker in Burien. I'm so sorry for your loss."

For an instant, I thought I saw some response on his face, but nothing more.

"She was also a hellion," Annie went on. "One day she tried to break everything in my office. I wrapped my arms around her to help her settle, but she broke free and pulled out a chunk of hair. I still have a bald spot."

Annie reached up and touched the right side of her head below her part, but any baldness was covered by fine blond hair. "She was my favorite, but you two had such hard lives. I remember."

Emery's eyes fluttered and half opened. "I remember," he echoed. "You. She…" His lips were dry, and his thoughts slowed. A cup of crushed ice sat melting by his bedside, so Annie held it up to offer. He nodded and she helped him hold it and take a small amount. His Adam's apple moved up and down to swallow.

"I…worried. She lowered her medications. She always liked how it felt when she got speedy," he said in rusty voice. "She wouldn't raise the dose until she got in trouble. Usually with sex. Sometimes I could talk her into…" His words began to slur from the effort of speaking and stopped. Emery rolled his head to the side, away from us. "She got bad."

"When did you know she was getting bad?" Annie asked. "She was dressed…"

He didn't answer right away and turned back to look at me. "Night at the chapel." He struggled for words again, but I saw his body slacken as if he'd be holding on too long and letting go would be a relief.

My phone buzzed in my hip pocket and I pulled it out to check the caller before I silenced it. The screen read Bebe McCrae—the Goth Girl, as I still thought of her. I hoped she'd seen Laurel, as I looked from the phone to Emery, wanting to give my attention to both. After only a beat, I passed on the call. "That night," I repeated, trying get back to the story.

He looked at the phone in my hand. "The phone," he said.

"That can wait. The memorial…" I tried to lead him back, but his eyes went out of focus and he dropped away again. Then I remembered the phone call he'd gotten at the memorial on the sleek, rose-colored phone after he'd told me his phone had been stolen so many times on the street. I touched his arm hoping he could give us just a moment more. "Emery. Do you mean the phone at the memorial?"

It was too late. His color and breathing seemed okay but he seemed to have used up all his energy.

"I'll ring for a nurse," Annie said.

I nodded my head hopelessly and showed my phone to Annie.

Bebe's name was still displayed. "I'm going to call back. It he wakes up, ask him if he had Marion's phone."

I pressed "call back" before I got to the hallway and huddled near the wall just outside Emery's door. "This is Grace," I said as soon as Bebe picked up. I realized she didn't even know that Annie was back, but before I could say more, her voice, loud and serious, came on.

"I saw Laurel. She was here."

"At her apartment?"

"Yes. She looked awful."

"Did you talk to her?"

"She took off. I don't know where. She has a parking place for her car around here somewhere. I think she's going to her mother's. I saw knives."

"She had knives?" I nearly screamed before I realized I was standing in a hospital hallway and the RN was entering Emery's room.

"No," Bebe said. "In my mind, I saw them. Something bad is going to happen."

I remembered Bebe saying that she knew things. I didn't know if I wanted that to be true or not, but I had to find out.

"I have her mother's phone number and I tried to call. There was no answer."

"I can call the restaurant," I said.

"I did that too. Her mother took the day off to work at home."

"Okay," I said. "I'll do something." I had no idea what.

I rounded the doorway back to Emery's room.

The nurse was checking the machines and glanced up. "He's fine. It's good that he's starting to wake up."

"Thank you," I said and pulled Annie into the hall to tell her what Bebe had said. She blanched.

"I'm okay," she said when I reacted with a look of concern.

"I'm going," I said and dug Mo James' address out of my bag.

Annie looked at it over my shoulder. "Long drive," she said and gripped me by both arms as if she wouldn't let me go. Her eyes squeezed shut and I imagined her seeing past trauma, but when she opened them, she was calm.

"I'll call Nate. We want police out there, but not just anyone."

I knew she was thinking about a young woman with mental illness we'd known. She had been shot and killed by the police. They'd been called to her apartment many times, but that day, an officer who didn't know her had responded. She did have knives.

"Try to find out if Emery came in with a phone." I said as I turned to leave.

"If they'll tell me," Annie said.

She was calm and so confident she seemed to radiate a glow like the saints I'd seen on her holy cards. That last image of Annie stayed with me like the final frame of a movie as I ran down the hall.

Chapter 26

Mo James' address was on Mt Si Road, a place I knew well from spring hikes Frank and I took on the famously steep and busy trail there. The light on James Street by the hospital was long enough to type the address into my phone so I'd know which place was hers. Everything out there had some acreage. The voice on Maps said my arrival time was in 25 minutes which sounded right for the middle of the night, but afternoon traffic was picking up.

The freeway rushed under my tires. On I-90 going over Lake Washington, the cold gray water was still choppy, and the pavement swayed under the car. My phone rang on the car's speaker and I hit the button to pick up.

"It's Nate."

"Are you coming?" I asked.

"Just now. I'll be right behind you. Give me the address."

I told him.

"Grace. I want you to wait until I get there. A gardener around the corner from Laurel's apartment found the knife that killed Marion Warfield. It was in some shrubs. A cop friend who hunts said they use that kind in slaughter. To bleed the animals."

"You're thinking Mo."

"Mo's the one with the carnivore restaurant. There were fingerprints. We don't have the results yet, but they seem to belong to a woman." Nate cleared his throat. "Grace, tell me you'll hang back when you get to North Bend. I go in first with the sheriff. When it's safe to come I'll let you know."

I was over the floating bridge now and on Mercer Island, the rich green suburb. The sky and the freeway were unbroken gray, bordered by evergreens—like I was in a steely chute speeding toward North Bend. I thought of the abandoned slaughterhouse at Northern State that read *You are among the forgotten.*

"I'll wait for you along Mount Si Road," I told Nate, but wondered if I would.

I'd learned long ago that I didn't want to make people worry about me. I didn't tell Frank about every situation I encountered at work. It stressed him out. I'd assess the situation at Mo's when I got there. Maybe nothing would happen. I told myself I was looking for a young woman who escaped from a psychiatric unit. That's all.

We hung up and I drove on but couldn't stop my thoughts from replaying the spilled blood in front of Laurel's apartment. Mo learned butchering from her father. It saved her from being raped and damned her to being a killer. But what about Laurel?

At the exit to North Bend, I sped through the round-about and the town's business district, the famous setting of Twin Peaks. I didn't even care if I got a speeding ticket passing through the small town. My tires squealed and I smelled rubber when I made the left turn onto Mo's road just after town. Mount Si loomed ahead—a few thousand feet of rocky incline jutting above evergreen forest. It was like the moon crashed to earth—just as the Snoqualmie Indian legend explained it. Mount Si's rocky man-in-the-moon face gazed upward. When my phone announced my destination, the peak shadowed the fenced pastures fronting Mo James' stone house just as she'd said.

A long, paved driveway ran between wire fences on either side. A dozen bearded goats grazed near a wood of skinny alder that skirted the property. I saw Mo and Laurel, both dressed in workman-like coveralls, behind the house at a board and batten shed, gesturing in an intense conversation that worried me. That was when I made the decision to come closer. I wanted to see more and hoped Nate wasn't far behind. The women didn't look up when I came nearer. I realized the Prius was silently running on battery. The driveway curved to a pullout where the house blocked them from view. I left the car there, intending to watch from the corner of the house, but before I rounded the edge, a rifle crack rang out. Without thinking about danger, I ran.

I heard a guttural wail. Behind me, the goats screamed. Who would I find down, Mo or Laurel? I didn't want to see either. Then I was there. A black and white guinea hog was splayed in the corral; stunned, with a dark hole above its eyes. Another hog and a flock of hens in the pen scattered and the red rooster flapped against the shed trying to flee. Mo leaned the rifle against the shed and leapt into the enclosure. She wasn't disheveled today. She wore her slash of red lipstick to a slaughter. How had I come upon this reenactment of Marion's death? How had Laurel? I watched the mother and daughter work. Their dance was practiced, but Laurel's mouth moved in a constant, silent commentary.

To my right, at the edge of the woods, a propane tank hissed under a blue, metal barrel of water, a block and tackle held meat hooks overhead. The hog was some sort of pygmy, no taller than my dog, Caesar, but probably weighed in near 200 pounds. Mo grabbed it by a jowl and held it down with her knee. Its hind legs kicked in spasm. Laurel was in the corral too, a plastic bowl and wooden spoon under her arm. Together they controlled the hog's involuntary bucking on the ground. Its speckled belly looked vulnerable.

Mo pulled a wood handled knife from a sheath on her belt and cut from side to side on the throat, hitting both arteries. A gaping smile opened in the neck and bloomed red. In perfect timing, Laurel placed the bowl to catch and stir the blood. I thought she moved on muscle memory; the job didn't require her mind to engage. The metallic scent of blood made me gag.

Both women looked up and finally saw me. Mo waved to the left. "Get the gate," she said, businesslike, as if the situation were normal.

Like Laurel, I moved without thinking and lifted the wire loop that fastened it to the fence. Between them, the two solidly built women hefted the dead hog and carried it to a pallet in front of the scalding barrel, Mo at the front feet, Laurel at the back. I closed the gate behind them. Mo glanced at me as Laurel lowered the gambrel with dangling hooks. "The man who usually helps couldn't come."

"You asked Laurel in his place?" I said, but thinking, *you already knew where Laurel was.* Watching them, images of the night of the murder with Laurel already in the throes of psychosis, working alongside her mother as she had so many times before. Mother and daughter had killed Marion Warfield. Now they knelt by the downed hog.

"I need help," Mo answered. She cut notches above the feet and placed the knife back in its sheath. I recognized the process; I'd helped a friend on his farm.

I might have felt relieved that the shot I heard was only part of farm work, the work that supplied the meat-heavy menu, but I watched in horror at Mo's cold bloodedness. The bizarre re-enactment of the therapist's murder showed me that Mo valued human life no more than meat. I flashed on the night of the killing. The three women at a therapy session with Mo's history of murder revealed. Laurel already believed she saw demons.

In revulsion at Mo's act, I wished I could confront her, but knew this was the wrong time.

Laurel looked up at me. Nothing about the young woman showed malice or motive to kill, but her thoughts could be exploited. Her eyes pleaded and her lips moved, but she returned her focus to the animal on the pallet. Her tan coveralls were stained with blood, dark and clotting, like the night when her clothing was covered with Marion Warfield's blood. Laurel may have participated in murder, but Mo was culpable.

They set the two hooks that would hoist the animal into the scalding water.

"Laurel needs to go back to treatment," I said, sure now it would be in the legal system, not the hospital. I knew the slaughter wouldn't be interrupted, but set a hook of my own, hoping the idea could take hold.

The young woman looked up and I realized I'd spoken as if she weren't present.

"I'm sorry, Laurel. You do."

"The hospital doesn't help," she said and looked around the barnyard with some confusion.

"This doesn't help," I said motioning to the slaughter in front of us. I wanted to present the pieces that had fallen into place, that Laurel's clothing was covered in Marion Warfield's blood, that the knife found in the bushes near where Marion was murdered had a woman's fingerprints. I hadn't wanted to believe Laurel would kill and still didn't. Now I forced myself to wait until Nate had arrived before I dug for the rest of the story.

My eyes shifted restlessly from the rifle leaning against the barn to the knife on Mo's belt. I thought of Jimmy James, Laurel's father. He wasn't the only one who interfered with their daughter's treatment.

"Mo," I said. I wanted to learn more. "Killing Angel was self-defense. He brought the knife. How could you keep that secret for so many years?"

Mo raised the hog and left it suspended over the barrel. Her stance showed every muscle tensed and almost trembling. "All I wanted was a new life. I ran. But every night, I'd fall asleep then jerk awake, see him on me again, see the knife, again and again. So, I put it behind me. My father, the scams. The boy." She visibly calmed herself. All her muscles relaxed. "I worked and worked and never slept. I never dreamed again." Mo wiped her face with the back of her hand. "How could I raise Laurel if I went to jail?"

I was struck by her ability to wall off the past even as she replicated the killing again and again on the farm. I knew that people didn't form the attachments to animals they raised for meat. It would be impossible to kill them. I supposed that was how Mo had lived, but it made me sad.

Laurel made a guttural noise that reminded me of the hog. "I had a dream once when I was a kid, that you killed a man the way you did the animals."

"No," Mo said. "I protected you..."

The sound of a car in the driveway grabbed our attention and I looked for Nate, but it was Jimmy James in a dented, blue Volvo. He passed the pullout by the house and drove up to the wire corral. I was relieved to see him, at least. He killed the engine and jumped out, leaving the door open behind him. Even in the cool air, Jimmy wore just a white shirt, sleeves rolled up and displaying the tattoos on his muscled arms.

I was between Jimmy and Mo. It seemed a bad place to be, but before I could step aside, he stopped. No one moved. The gravel yard outside the corral suddenly felt small.

Mo's glare was chilling, a glare that took in Jimmy, and me too. She stepped toward us, her hand moving toward the knife sheathed on her belt. Laurel moved like a specter by the barn. A brightness at the edge of my vision distorted their actions.

"Stop," I said, counting on Jimmy to help in his drive to protect Laurel. A knife flashed in his hand too and he moved toward me. Mo and Laurel had seen this. I hadn't.

"Stop," I said again, realizing how often, in my work, I said this calmly, firmly, and successfully. People stopped.

I had been all wrong about the murder. Today, Mo stopped, but not Jimmy. He grabbed my hair, his knuckles grinding into my head. I fell back into his chest, off balance. His smell was sharp. I felt the cold blade touch my throat. He released my hair and held me to him with his forearm.

Even slowed by medications and distracted by her thoughts, Laurel reached the rifle, pulled the now tattered gauze from her injured fingers, and hefted it to her shoulder, pointing at Jimmy.

It was Mo who spoke. "Laurel, put the gun down. You don't want to kill." Her voice was weary.

Chapter 27

It was like being in a car accident. In the moments before a crash, time slows. An entire lifetime can pass in those moments. The wind turned cold and blew a veil of clouds over the face of Mount Si. Before it disappeared, I looked at its rocky surface, hoping for strength. Jimmy pressed one arm into my sternum, in his other, he still held the knife at my throat. Nate had told me to wait for him. I wondered how far he was and if his arrival would help—or push events forward to their worst conclusion.

Laurel held the rifle steady but her voice waivered. "That's how you held Marion. She was dressed like a demon." Then Laurel whispered, "Stop it," but not to us. She pulled her attention back to the moment. "That night after the session, you showed up. You grabbed her hair and put the knife to her throat. I ran to her and pulled your hand to stop it, but I felt the knife move, the tendons crack. It was too late. Then Marion moaned and fell."

Laurel's voice was high and fast. "You told me you only meant to scare her—so close to Halloween, you said. You told me that I took the knife and killed her."

Finally, I learned what happened. Not Mo, but Jimmy with a knife to Marion's throat.

"Laurel," I said, so she'd know she was heard, "You told Annie that you killed Marion, but you didn't."

"You made me think I did it, Jimmy. The voices were so loud already. They started screaming from the doorway, the parked cars, every part of the street. A million voices telling me I killed Marion. It was you, my own father. Over and over, you told me I killed her. You described how I did it again and again, just close enough to what really happened."

"Then you ran," she said to her father.

He did not answer.

"You killed her. You killed her." Laurel repeated, as if to make up for the number of times he'd told her the opposite.

Jimmy shifted his balance. "I'm still not sure you remember it right, Sweetie. I only want to help. Your thinking is distorted."

"By you," Laurel said. "You can't convince me twice. You're a con man just like my grandfather. Are you trying to send me to jail? The only person you help is yourself." She fanned the fingers that held the gun barrel. Without the dirty gauze, lines of pink skin opened and bled.

"You cut me too."

Then I remembered that Jimmy had been meeting someone at his gigs. "You knew Marion Warfield," I said. "She was the woman who came to hear you play every night."

I felt his hot breath as he spoke.

"I didn't mean for it to turn out that way, Laurel honey," he said as if she had asked instead of me. "You wanted me to go to a family session with you, so I looked up your therapist, found out all about Marion Warfield. When I got to town, I tracked her down and followed her from her office. That's how I managed to meet her. I don't trust those people, Laurel. You know what they did to my son."

Jimmy shifted his weight, pulling me off balance too. The knife nicked my skin and I seemed to leave my body. I watched the scene from far away, safe on Mount Si.

"Marion was this crazy, sexy woman," Jimmy said. "She started coming to the clubs every night. She was wild—two different people. The one who wanted to poison you with medications, and the one who was so hot in bed."

"You slept with my therapist?" Laurel's voice cracked.

"She was just for fun. She was crazy, Laurel. Crazier than you."

"Marion helped me," Laurel said.

"She's all you ever talked about. *Marion this. Marion that.*" He made his voice high and mocking. *"Marion says get to know your father. Marion changed her mind and says he's not good for you. Marion says take your meds."* His voice lowered. "She didn't take her own meds. She liked the high. Here we go again. Another shrink pushing medicine, just like the ones who killed Jimmy Junior."

Jimmy tensed with anger and I was back in my body, because I needed to be there.

Laurel widened her stance. The gun was steady. Her lips no longer moved in response to voices. The crisis had cleared her thoughts, but I worried that continued stress would overwhelm her. I wondered what Jimmy's intent was. The horrible thought came that he was going to commit suicide by getting his daughter to shoot him.

"All you wanted was a replacement for Little Jimmy," she said. "Little You. You never saw who I was."

I reached for Jimmy's crushing arm and tried to release some pressure. My fingers covered the part of his tattoo that spelled out JJ, for his son. He'd written that loss on his body. He shifted his weight and held me tighter. He had lost Laurel too.

"What happened that night?" I asked to steer away from the conflict.

"My demon girl, your therapist, figured out who I was." Again, he directed his answer to Laurel. "She was done with you, honey. She was going to *terminate* you because of our conflict of interest." He said the word in a way that suggested other meanings. "But she didn't tell you that. She wanted this meeting with you and Mo."

Laurel stood, unmoving.

"She was a bad shrink, and Mo, you're a bad mother. I made a plan that would get rid of you both. Kill the demon and frame the mother. All I wanted was to take care of you, Laurel."

"You believe that you were doing it for me?" Laurel said.

I felt Jimmy's every breath as he restrained me.

On the mountain, the wind made a moaning sound like the Requiem at Marion's memorial. Fallen leaves scattered at our feet. Pressed against him, I could feel a bottomless, selfish need flow through him into me.

"Taking care of people" I said, trying to calm Jimmy. "It's your strength."

"All the people I helped. In the program. I was there for you, Laurel. I knew what to do."

Laurel reacted. "You never…"

I made a silent *shh* and gently shook my head, sending a look to Laurel pleading that she let him talk. I wanted time for Nate to arrive, time to think of some plan to free us all. Laurel didn't even seem to see me, but Mo did. She reached a hand toward Laurel.

"Listen, Laurel. I need to know what happened."

Jimmy wanted to talk. "Your therapist was a slut." Spittle sprayed over my shoulder when he spoke. "After Jimmy Junior, I wouldn't take it anymore. I wouldn't let her ruin you, Laurel, and the only way to stop her was to kill her. When your grandfather told me that Mo killed that boy, I knew how to do it."

Mo's face became mask-like. I noticed that she still had blood on her hands, but she didn't seem to see it. She touched her face and platinum hair as if to make sure she was still herself. "My knives were gone," she said.

"You talked me into showing you Mom's restaurant." Understanding showed on Laurel's face. "You planned it all and took the knives," Laurel said.

Jimmy removed the knife from my skin and wagged it. "Here's one. I slaughtered the demon girl. Just like your mother killed that pig and like she killed that boy. It tied together perfectly." Jimmy pressed the knife into my jaw again. I felt a warm ooze of blood on my neck. He'd broken skin. "But things went wrong. She was on her way to meet me. I meant to do it on campus where it was dark and quiet, but some event had ended, and people were everywhere. So, I followed her past Broadway to a quieter street. I didn't even know where you lived, Laurel, then you showed up. It was your apartment. A homeless guy saw it all. The whole fucking world was there."

The wind moaned again. I thought of all the deaths: Marion, Theo's brother, Jimmy's son. The mournfulness rang in my ears and I remembered Emery at the chapel, broken by sadness.

Remembered the phone. He was the homeless man. He found Marion's phone.

"The homeless man was Marion's brother. He took Marion's phone," I said. "And called you."

"He demanded to see me. What did he think would happen? We'd have a nice talk. He was sick like Marion. I told him to meet me in the same place. It turned out better, I saw him walking along 12th and it was Sunday night. Now, the place was empty. I drove my car into him. He made a terrible sound when he hit the hood." Jimmy seemed more moved by the sound than by any of the deaths. "Then I had to get away."

"You can get away now," I said and wondered if Jimmy knew that Emery was still alive. "There's still time for you to go, Jimmy."

"It's too late. There's only one way I'll get away now."

"Are you going to commit suicide?" I asked because my body stood between him and his daughter with the rifle. "Like Jimmy Junior? No…" My thoughts raced with ways to talk him down. I should be able to do this. It was what I did.

"I'm ready to be with Jimmy Junior and I'm taking you with me." He cut me off. At the same time his forearm moved up to my windpipe crushing me in a chokehold. His other arm added leverage to the hold. I knew I had only a moment to react before losing consciousness. No more waiting.

Time stopped again. Colors brightened. Sounds intensified. Very slowly, the memory of Calvin Cole, the gun shot, and Nate's fall unreeled in my mind as if whatever was about to happen had already been written. I wondered if it was fated for me to go through this again—and for the last time. I wanted to change the ending.

I tucked my chin to protect my airway. Pulled down on his wrist with one hand. Moving on to things I never learned in safety training at work, I made my other hand into a fist and swung it into his groin with as much force as I could. I connected. Jimmy doubled forward in surprise and pain. I elbowed his face and his grip released. I had no idea what was going on around me. I thought I heard cars in the driveway.

First the smell, then sound of a gunshot pierced the barnyard. The remaining pig in the corral screamed with fear and the rooster flapped its wings in terror. I pulled away from Jimmy and saw what had happened. Laurel had shot in the air and now she and Mo both moved toward Jimmy as if they had planned it. Laurel swung the rifle like a bat and connected with Jimmy's arm. He grunted in pain and released his grip on the knife. Mo scooped it up like she was fielding a ball. All three of us stepped back and Jimmy stood, hands empty.

At the same time, two cars spun up, past the house, and screeched to a stop. Nate and the sheriff. The doors of both cars flew open, and Nate ran toward us.

"Jimmy is the killer," I screamed, afraid they would misinterpret the rifle and the knife in the women's hands. The men tackled Jimmy and cuffed him. They collected the weapons and placed them in the trunk of the sheriff's car.

I started shaking.

Chapter 28

What was the story I wanted to tell?

That there was no murder. That Laurel learned to manage her illness and all the pain her family carried. That Marion, who also struggled with mental illness, lived to take better care of herself and others. That Theo's brother lived, and Mo didn't carry the guilt of his death. I would include something for Jimmy and Mo's father as well, but I wasn't sure what.

For myself, I wished that Annie and I would still work together, eating weekly prime rib and laughing. That Nell had a wonderful trip, then came back to a job with a boss who respected her. That we all found a way to live with our demons.

Instead, after the day in the shadow of Mount Si, I went to bed and stared at the ceiling where the cracks replayed the scene at Mo's farm. I understood Annie's trauma in a new way.

I woke up the next morning in tangled sheets. Frank's side of the bed was cold. My alarm clock said 11:59 and turned over to noon while I watched. Out the window, the sky was a pale unbroken gray, the kind that signals the change of season. The light would be low and fleeting from now on. It was Halloween.

Nell tiptoed upstairs with a mug of coffee. "My flight is tomorrow night," she said. "Can you help me finish packing?"

She was appealing to my guilt and my need to organize, trying to help me come back into the world. My head was heavy on the pillow and my eyes were gluey.

"You don't need me. I'll get up later and make dinner. What do you want?"

194

We agreed on Chicken Provençal and Nell went downstairs to pull a package of thighs from the freezer. I stayed in bed like my mom had all those years of my childhood. Paralyzed by fatigue.

The next time I woke, the edge of the bed sagged, and I opened my eyes to Frank there next to me. I'd told him everything about the night before. He picked up my hand. "Are you sick?"

I shook my head no and smelled the roasting chicken I hadn't gotten up to cook.

"It's Nell's last day home," Frank said his voice firm. "You've got to get up."

"I'm coming." I slowly pulled on a pair of jeans and the frayed t shirt I wore every morning. Downstairs, I splashed water on my face and brushed my hair. Just when I stepped out, Caesar barked and rushed to the front door.

Annie tapped on the glass. I opened the door, and she gave me a long hug like Frank had, her hair cool from the air outside.

"Are you okay?" she asked.

I wanted to be okay but wasn't. I shook my head. "No. I feel like I'm underwater."

"I knew it," she said and walked me into the kitchen and settled me at the table like an old woman.

I saw the eye contact passing between Annie, Frank, and Nell. They had been talking.

"Coffee or wine?" she asked but saw deciding even that was too much for me. "Coffee first, then wine with dinner."

I noticed the table was set for four. Frank took Annie's coat and handed her a glass of wine for herself.

"I called Nate," Annie said. "The detectives talked to Emery. He's getting better. Want to know what he said?"

It was the first thing that perked me up. I wanted to hear what happened.

"He saw everything the night Marion was killed. He planned to meet her after her last session to get a phone she'd bought for him. The garage at SU was closed and she'd parked by Laurel's apartment."

I pictured the dark street by Bebe's shop. "She was meeting Jimmy James after," I said. "She dressed the part."

"That's what I think too. It fit with Jimmy's story." Annie went on. "Anyway, Emery was down the block, walking to meet her, when he saw a man grab her. He ran toward them and yelled."

"Can he describe him?" I asked. "For court? I want Jimmy James put away."

"The big beard and slicked back hair, yes. But Jimmy's another story. He tried to hang himself in the back of the police car—so he's on suicide watch. He's talking now, admitting it all and blaming Marion for making him kill her. He was wronged as a father. Marion's murder was so well planned, though. He'd taken the knives from Mo, to frame her."

"I know. Did he put the squirrel on her door?"

"Yes. Along with Mo's con-artist father, Patrick, who brought it all the way from Conway. Her own father thought she was the murderer. Again."

"He came all the way to Duvall with a squirrel?"

"I think Mo's father wanted to punish her for keeping Laurel away all those years." Annie shrugged at the strangeness of trying to understand people's motivations.

We heard a car in the driveway. Caesar ran to the door, barking again. A father and a group of trick-or-treaters came to the door. We didn't get many out here. Frank let them choose candy bars that I hadn't remembered to buy. The kids politely took turns. The last two wore the crow costumes I'd seen in town. One cocked his cartoonish head and looked at me a long time. Then they yelled, "Thanks," and ran back to the car.

Nell cradled her wine glass in her hands, more confident with her new haircut. She took over the story. "I found Theo Martinez' phone number in your purse and called him. I wanted him to know it was over, in case that old anger had him following Mo again. He wasn't angry, Mom. He cried."

Sadness washed over me too. "Maybe he can say good-bye to his brother now. Thanks for doing that. I wonder what will happen to Mo?"

"She'd have quite a case for self-defense, but Theo has no intention of taking her to the police," Nell said.

Frank, in a faded and stained burgundy chef's apron, brought a platter heaped with chicken from the stove.

"Thanks for doing this," I said. "All of you."

If anything could rekindle my appetite, it was the smell of roasted chicken fat scented with herbs and lemon. Nell carried potatoes and vegetables to the table and passed them. I helped myself to a small portion and she gave me a stern look. I took a little more. Everyone was hovering.

"You didn't finish talking about Emery," Nell prompted Annie.

"By the time he got there, Jimmy was gone, and his sister was down. No pulse. He grabbed her purse and ran."

"Why didn't he go to the police?" Nell made a judging face, but I understood his decision.

"Marion was gone," I said using a euphemism. "He still had to survive on the streets. He wanted the phone and the cash. So, he had Marion's iPhone."

"He figured out how to unlock it," Annie continued, "and got an eye full of explicit photos of Marion with Jimmy. The night of the memorial he dialed the number she had been calling from her phone. I don't know what he thought he was going to do, but that's when Jimmy plowed over him with his car. The police have the damaged car. Jimmy didn't even know Emery was still alive."

"What about Laurel?" Nell asked. "Is she going back to the hospital?"

"She's there now. Thankfully, not in jail. That's what would have happened with Jimmy's plan. Her instead of him. Nice Dad. Laurel has a lot to sort out once her medications are stabilized. At least she knows what really happened." Annie took a bite of chicken and nodded at the taste. "It's good."

"Grace's recipe," Frank said as if I could take credit for anything today.

"Mo wants Laurel to stay with her in North Bend," Annie continued.

I shuddered. "I hate to think of her staying at Mo's house in the shadow of Mount Si after all that happened there."

"She won't go," Annie said. "I went to see Bebe McCrae. She

had the mop out again. She's already talked to Laurel and got her permission to help clean the apartment—the kitchen and old food for now. Then they'll tackle the desk and walls together. Bebe didn't even seem surprised when I told her what happened at the butchering."

Which didn't surprise me.

Annie reached into her pocket, pulled out something small and shiny and rolled it to me.

I scooped up the glass eye with its sky-blue iris and held it on my palm for Frank and Nell to see. "Bebe has a dish full of these in her shop—from a doll factory. I admired them."

"She said you'd like it," Annie said.

I looked around the table at my family and friend who had conspired to get me out of bed and to the table. Annie picked up the platter of chicken and instead of passing it for second helpings, gave me another serving with a look that told me to eat more. She would be a good nun.

We carried the dirty dishes to the sink, but Frank insisted we leave them there. Nell, Annie, and Frank did the eye contact thing again. "We have something else planned."

He touched my shoulder to guide me to the back door. "We set up a bonfire out back."

"No," I said. Food and talk had brought another wave of exhaustion. "I got out of bed for dinner, but I'm not up for this."

Nell caught my eye. She looked strong and serious. "It's a ritual."

"Oh honey, I saw the book on grief was out again, but I..."

"Just come. If you want, all you have to do is sit."

I pulled my coat from the peg by the back door. Annie and I went first, carrying our glasses and the wine bottle. Nell last. She let the screen door slam and I winced involuntarily. The moon had risen behind the trees. At Nell's cottage the ginkgoes had dropped all their leaves at the same moment and a pool of gold covered the ground. We reached the clearing and the stone ring where we burned blowdowns and debris. They had already set up wood teepee-style with crumpled paper and kindling at its feet. Patio chairs circled the fire pit.

Nell caught up, carrying the suitcase from Northern State.

My first thought was that we would be burning Lucy's things, then I smiled, realizing it was just me still avoiding. It was time to look. I liked the idea of opening the suitcase outside, free of my grandparents' judgement. We'd had enough demons in recent days.

Caesar stuck by my side, his ruff up, still protecting me from the emotional charge of the contents. I wasn't sure if I was afraid of what I'd find or afraid I'd find nothing at all. Frank handed me the kitchen matches and I lit the fire. The newsprint turned orange, then black and the edges curled in a lace of ash. The dried twigs snapped as they caught fire. The smell of smoke smudged the air.

We stared at the hypnotic flames. It seemed like enough ritual for me.

"The fire is to chase the evil spirits away," Annie said. She wore a gray wool coat with big cuffs and held her hands together as if in prayer.

"Isn't this a little pagan for you?" I asked.

"Nell's idea," she said.

"Well, we talked about it." Nell said, and set the suitcase next to me. "It's like Day of the Dead. These days around Halloween are when the veil is lifted between this world and the next."

"The church celebrates All Souls," Annie said.

"Exactly," Nell agreed.

Frank motioned to the suitcase. "I got it open," he said, "but I promise we haven't looked."

"You've been busy." I said, warmed by the fire and their concern.

"Open it," Nell said finally.

I was about to ask for more light, but a nearly full moon and the fire were enough.

I slid the brass clasps open. Inside, I lifted out the few items: a folded green dress with a matching belt, a good dress, as if Lucy had put on her Sunday clothes for her last trip away from home; a pair of pumps and a handbag; peach colored lipstick that after so many years still smelled flowery. At the bottom, a pair of pearlized cat-eye glasses lay folded on top of an envelope.

"They didn't let Lucy have her glasses?" I said, outraged and fearing that she was either too debilitated by her illness or the treatment to use them. I set them carefully aside. The letter had been opened, at least she'd gotten that. I read my mother's careful grade school script out loud—*Dear Mom, I hope you feel better soon. I'm cleaning my room every day and helping Auntie with the dishes. We can cook together when you come home, whatever you like. Love, Rose.* Below, she had drawn elaborate pictures of roses in orange and yellow crayon swirls.

Nell leaned in and traced the drawing with a finger. "It's the peaches and cream rose. Grandma's favorite from her garden."

"My favorite too," I said. "Maybe it was originally Grandma Lucy's rose. Is that possible?"

"If we want it to be." Nell said.

I nodded, thinking about how we'd never know the real stories. I'd have to be satisfied with making my own meaning.

Annie pulled us back to the ceremony and Frank shared memories of my mom.

"Who are we saying good-bye to, my mom or Lucy?" I asked.

His eyebrows went up.

"Oh," I said, *"All* the souls."

I thought of Marion Warfield, a perfect example of a person who deserved to rest in peace in spite of, or because of, her problems. I thought of Laurel's family, the boy Mo killed, Jimmy's son. I wished them well too.

In the distance, I heard a chorus of high-pitched honking moving closer, growing louder, and melding into a roar. The snow geese were overhead. The light from the moon reflected on their white bodies as they passed in one V formation after another. I'd heard that they honk to keep the flock in formation when they travel. Like the geese, Nell and Annie were leaving, I thought, but we would still be connected. The sound of the migration just overhead, pulled me too. I wouldn't go along, but I hoped I could move forward.

Here at home, Frank and I would go to visit Grandma Lucy's grave at Northern State. We could dig up the peaches and cream rose from my mother's house and plant it at the corner of our porch where it would get sun and care.

I remembered the morning we scattered Mom's ashes. I still didn't know what to say, but decided to try. No one cared if my words were imperfect. I poured a little more wine all around and spoke. "Here's to Mom. Now I know her in a new way and it's time for me to learn to forgive her." I talked about the people who had died and the people who were leaving. I talked about how, for those of us at the bonfire, our stories weren't over yet. We wouldn't be able to change what happened to a happy ending, but we could, at least, try to stop keeping secrets.

"Maybe the geese will be in the fields by the Snoqualmie River in the morning." I said.

Reading Group Guide
Questions for Discussion

1. *Danger to Others* is bracketed by rituals in first and last chapters. In the beginning, Grace and her family go to spread her mother's ashes. At the end of the book, Nell, Annie and Frank plan a bonfire. How do these rituals affect Grace? Have you planned events like these? Is one memorial enough?

2. What is the importance of food in *Danger to Others*: Nell's pancakes; Mo, now a restauranteur, doing scams to feed her brothers and sisters and saying, "my whole life was about feeding people." Do you remember other places food was mentioned as meaningful?

3. "Justice means giving each person what he or she deserves or, in more traditional terms, giving each person his or her due." (Markkula Center for Applied Ethics) Theo says, "What I want is some kind of justice." In the wake of what happened to his brother, what would that look like to him? What would justice be for Mo? For Laurel's father? For Nate and the traumatized professionals?

4. How does the author use the time of year, the setting and the natural world to reflect the story's themes?

5. What does the image of demons that appears in Laurel's hallucinations, Nell's art books and Marion Warfield's dress mean to you? Is this image historic or does it still have meaning today?

6. Annie and Grace (and other characters as well) have reactions to traumas they experienced in their personal lives. How do their ways of coping serve or fail them?

7. How do unspoken events in families affect them? Do family members sometimes act in ways that reflect those secrets, without even knowing it? Have you discovered anything like this in your family?

About the Author

Martha Crites has worked in both community and inpatient mental health for many years and taught at the Quileute Tribal School on the Washington coast. When she isn't working and writing, you will find her working in her garden or walking and volunteering on the Camino de Santiago, the medieval pilgrimage trail in Spain. Her first novel, *Grave Disturbance*, was a finalist for the Pacific Northwest Writers Association's Nancy Pearl Award. Her short work has been featured in the anthology, *Camino de Santiago: a spiritual companion* (Redemptorist Publications). She lives with her husband and her somewhat wild Labrador retriever in Seattle, Washington. Martha is a member of Mystery Writers of America and Sisters in Crime.